SHADOWS OF REGRET

SHADOWS OF REGRET

Julie Coffin

Chivers Press • G.K. Hall & Co.
Bath, England Thorndike, Maine USA

This Large Print edition is published by Chivers Press, England, and by G.K. Hall & Co., USA.

Published in 2000 in the U.K. by arrangement with the author.

Published in 2000 in the U.S. by arrangement with Julie Coffin.

U.K. Hardcover ISBN 0-7540-4200-6   (Chivers Large Print)
U.K. Softcover ISBN 0-7540-4201-4   (Camden Large Print)
U.S. Softcover ISBN 0-7838-9095-8   (Nightingale Series Edition)

The text of this Large Print edition is unabridged.
Other aspects of the book may vary from the original edition.

Set in 16 pt. New Times Roman.

Printed in Great Britain on acid-free paper.

British Library Cataloguing in Publication Data available

Library of Congress Cataloging-in-Publication Data

Coffin, Julie.
    Shadows of regret / Julie Coffin.
        p. cm. — (G.K. Hall large print nightingale series)
    ISBN 0-7838-9095-8 (lg. print : sc : alk. paper)
    1. Cornwall (England : County)—Fiction. 2. Nannies—Fiction.
    3. Large type books. I. Title. II. Series.
    PR6053.O3 S53 2000
    823'.914—dc21   00–039532

CHAPTER ONE

The cry was a thin, pathetic trail of sound weaving its way round her. Even before she was properly awake, Linzi slid her feet over the side of the bed and stumbled towards the adjoining room.

Jonathan lay in his cot, sleeping peacefully, one, small thumb tucked into his mouth, his rounded cheeks softly flushed with colour in the faint glow of the bedside lamp. Puzzled, Linzi stared down at him.

He's beautiful, she thought, her hand smoothing lights across his silken hair as she tucked the covers a little more closely round him. Neither of the children she'd been nanny to before had been quite as perfect or contented as this one.

For a moment Linzi paused, listening to the faint rhythm of his breathing, then crept back into her own room again, leaving the door slightly ajar.

And yet there had been a cry. She was certain of that. A long-drawn-out fretful wail, like that of a newborn child. Even now the sound seemed to hang in the air, haunting her.

But there were no other babies staying in the house—only Jonathan.

Linzi snuggled down under the duvet, her toes exploring the chillier corners of the bed

1

until she drew them back and curled herself into a tight ball. Moonlight flooded in through one corner of the window, where the curtains didn't quite reach the wall, creating shadows. The snow outside gave it a curious brightness.

Even with her eyes shut, she could visualise the room, high-ceilinged, its mullioned windows edged with grey stone ledges; the furniture of heavy dark wood, polished over the years to a deep sheen, lining its plain white walls.

It still amazed her that she could be here, in such a place—a house filled with so much history. Since she'd become Jonathan's nanny, her life had changed completely.

She let her mind travel back to September...

'Gavin and I are both solicitors,' Morwenna Breage had explained, pushing one hand through her dark fringe so that it stood up in thin spikes, before falling like a waterfall over her forehead again. 'And I've been working on stuff for him at home ever since Jonathan was born. It's Gavin's firm, you see, so that makes things easier.' She clutched wildly at the baby as he made a grab for the coffee mug sitting on the table nearby.

'Gavin's a bit old-fashioned in a way. Wives should stay at home and look after their offspring—you know the sort of thing.' She laughed. 'It's his mother's fault. She rules his whole family with a rod of iron. We're all terrified of her!'

2

Morwenna pushed the empty mug out of her son's reach, then continued. 'Working at home wasn't too bad at first, what with Jonathan sleeping most of the time, but now he's becoming more mobile . . .' She hugged the baby to her as she spoke and kissed the top of his smooth head. 'He's just started to pull himself upright and stagger round holding on to the furniture, so I spend most of my time keeping one eye on him—which doesn't exactly improve my concentration.'

Restraining Jonathan's exploring fingers, Morwenna rapidly scanned through the pages of Linzi's cv. 'You've the National Nursery Examination Board certificate, I see,' she commented, 'and had two jobs already. Why change?'

Linzi smiled. 'The first was only temporary, looking after a two-year-old. Her parents were French and came from Brittany,' she explained. 'They were over here on a business trip for a month. The family owned vineyards and were trying to find new markets for their wine in the British Isles. I travelled with them.'

'Did you enjoy it?'

Linzi nodded. 'I certainly learned a great deal about my own country—and improved my French, too. Gabriella and I were both bilingual by the time they returned to Brittany again.'

'I don't think Jonathan's quite up to a second language yet, are you, my poppet?'

3

Morwenna chuckled. 'He is beginning to talk though. Just the occasional word or two. What about your present job?'

'That's been for almost a year. Thomas's mother, Lucy, returned to work when he was six weeks old, but became pregnant again a few months later. Her husband's a very successful accountant, and now the second baby's arrived Lucy's decided to take a year or so off to bring up the children herself. She's a social worker, you see, and thinks it might give her a better insight into the problems of coping with a family.' Linzi gave a doleful smile. 'So I'm afraid I'm out of a job again.'

The trill of the telephone interrupted their conversation and while Morwenna Breage leaned over to answer it, Jonathan lunged forward to seize the quivering plastic of the cord in both dimpled fists. Swiftly, and before the instrument plummeted from the shelf, Linzi whisked him from his mother's arm, talking soothingly to him as she did so, then carried him over to the high window overlooking the slow-moving grey of the Thames far below.

After a first startled look at her, while his bottom lip trembled ominously, Jonathan's mouth curved into a wide smile, revealing four, tiny, white teeth, and his gaze followed the river-boat Linzi was pointing out to him.

'Sorry about that,' Morwenna apologised, when the phone call was over. 'But you see what I mean now, don't you? He's into everything. Even so, I shall hate being apart from him,' she said regretfully. 'Now, how about some more coffee while we discuss when you can start?'

A fortnight later, Linzi moved into the Breage's beautiful Docklands flat to begin her new life. The job was a pleasure to her. Jonathan was a delightful baby, full of smiles and always placid. A welcome contrast to Thomas, her previous charge.

Morwenna and her husband, Gavin, insisted that, when they were at home in the evenings and at week-ends, Linzi should have the time free to do as she wished. So, living in London for the first time, after a childhood spent in Sussex, she made the most of it, seeing every stage-show she could and visiting all the exhibitions and art galleries. The salary she earned was generous and, living with the family as she did, her expenses were few.

Life, Linzi decided blissfully, couldn't be more perfect. And then Morwenna told her of their arrangements for Christmas.

'That was Gavin's mother on the phone,' Morwenna said, with a rather rueful expression on her usually cheerful face, as she came into the bathroom where Linzi was giving Jonathan his evening bath. 'She lives in this enormous, old house down in the West Country. It's been in the family for centuries and since Gavin's father died a few years back, she's run it as a hotel. It's the only way she can afford to keep it going, and she refuses to part with the place. Not that any of us would want her to—it's fantastic.'

Morwenna scooped up her laughing son and hugged him into a thick white towel, while Linzi let the water drain away.

'Each year she closes the hotel and invites the whole lot of us there for Christmas. You won't mind, will you?'

'Sounds exciting,' Linzi replied, retrieving a yellow duck from the fast-disappearing water, and sitting it on the bath-rack.

Morwenna's face clouded.

'Well . . . I'm not too sure about that,' she said doubtfully. 'It's right on the edge of the sea, miles from anywhere, windswept and bleak in winter—and my mother-in-law is a dragon.'

Linzi took Jonathan from her and began to towel dry him, then expertly put on his nappy.

'How do you make it look so easy?' Morwenna sighed, watching her. 'I always seem to end up with an arm and a leg tucked inside when he squirms about like that.'

'Is Gavin's family large?' Linzi enquired, deftly slipping the baby's kicking feet into his pale-blue night-suit. 'You said "the whole lot of us". How many go?'

Morwenna ran her finger through a trail of talcum powder on the side of the bath. 'His two sisters never miss. And Claire has a horde of children. Well, half of them are Philip's from his first marriage—although I suppose they might spend Christmas with their own mother, unless she's going skiing like last year,' she mused, wrinkling up her nose. 'And Eve has a five-year-old who's a little beast—just started school and it seems to have brought the worst out in him. He was pretty awful before, too.'

She bent to kiss her son's flushed cheek. 'You'll never be like that, will you, darling?' Morwenna lifted Jonathan and carried him into his bedroom, her voice continuing, 'And probably Gavin's younger brother . . . Alex . . . will be there.'

Linzi noticed a slight hesitation as she said the name, and wondered why. But before she could ask, Morwenna's voice, singing the words of a nursery rhyme, floated back to her as she tidied up the bathroom.

'Out like a light at last,' Morwenna sighed, when she eventually came back and they made their way to the stop of the stairs. 'So who's the lucky guy you're seeing tonight, Lin?'

Linzi grinned wryly. 'You make it sound as though I have dozens of them, lined up and waiting.'

'Haven't you?' Morwenna teased.

'It would be nice.'

'So it's still Ardent Andy then?'

Regretfully, Linzi nodded. She'd sat next to Andrew at a concert in the Festival Hall and when they started chatting during the interval, found they shared a similar taste in music. Since then, however, she'd discovered they had nothing else in common, but found it difficult to break off their relationship. Like Linzi, Andrew lived away from his family and had few, if any, friends in London. And at concerts, she did enjoy his company.

'Well, don't let him whisk you away to some cosy little love-nest yet, will you?' Morwenna observed. 'I don't know what we'd do without you.'

'Don't worry,' Linzi replied. 'Jonathan's the only love of my life at the moment.'

'Thank goodness for that!' Morwenna laughed, reaching the bottom step and heading towards the kitchen. 'From all the clatter, it sounds as though Gavin's grown impatient and started dishing up the evening meal. We'd better not keep him waiting any longer.'

*　　*　　*

When they left London, early on the morning of Christmas Eve, snow had been falling for several hours. By then it was turning to slush on the pavements; and drifting into grubby, speckled heaps in the gutters. A grey sky hung like dull pewter over the steadily whitening countryside as the miles sped away, and the car's windscreen wipers droned to and fro, trying to clear the filthy build-up of spattered spray accumulating from the slushy, wet roads.

Jonathan slept for most of the journey, his small head lolling sideways against the padded seat-rest; his thumb tucked as usual into his mouth, making tiny sucking noises every now and then. In the heat of the car, Linzi felt drowsy, too, struggling to keep her eyes open.

They stopped for lunch at an old pub on the outskirts of Salisbury, where one of the barmaids cheerfully heated up a couple of Jonathan's jars of baby-food and provided a high chair, while the rest of them tucked in to thick gammon steaks liberally garnished with rounds of pineapple, huge open mushrooms, slices of juicy tomato and jacket potatoes oozing butter. By the time they'd finished off the meal with chocolate gateau, snow was already freezing on the car windscreen and it took Gavin several minutes to scrape it clear.

The afternoon had darkened when they crossed the Tamar bridge into Cornwall and without Gavin pointing out that below stretched the wide river, Linzi would never have realised it was even there.

A few miles after that, Morwenna took over the driving to give her husband a rest. As Gavin turned his head to smile his thanks, Linzi saw his face in the glow from the dashboard and thought that despite being quite a few years older than his wife, he was still an extremely attractive man. It was at times like this that she envied their obvious happiness with each other.

'OK, Lin?' he asked, twisting round in his seat to speak to her. 'Another hour or so and we should be there.'

'Providing this weather eases off a bit,' Morwenna remarked grimly, slowing the car to a crawl. 'Can you keep a look out for our turn off, darling? That last signpost was impossible to read.'

The last few miles grew increasingly difficult. Drifts had formed, reaching almost from bank to bank of the narrow lane, making every bend a hazard. Snow slithered from over-laden branches to land with a dull thud on the roof, making Linzi jump, and she could only admire Morwenna's expert handling of the car.

It seemed to Linzi that the lane would never end, but suddenly the headlights revealed tall stone pillars and Gavin climbed swiftly out. The snow buried his shoes as he tugged at the heavy wrought-iron gates, then returned quickly, rubbing his cold hands.

'I hope the central heating's working after that recent bit of rebuilding,' he growled, hunching himself down in the seat again, his breath misting the windscreen in front of him as he leaned forward to brush the snow from his jacket. 'It was right above the lounge and that room's the size of a barn—and murder to keep warm.'

'I shouldn't worry, darling,' Morwenna

comforted, her eyes scanning the road ahead. 'Your mother always has such enormous log fires in every room, the heating's not really needed at all. Do you remember last year when we had to open the windows, it was so hot?'

'That was last year, Wenna. We even found violets blooming under the hedges then, Lin— but we haven't had snow like this for years, especially not down here in Cornwall.'

Jonathan had woken when the car door slammed shut, and was restless. The darkness worried him, and Linzi spent the last part of the journey trying to keep him amused so that he didn't cry. Morwenna has enough to do controlling the car in these treacherous conditions, she reasoned, without a baby niggling in the background.

The driveway seemed to go on for miles, snow-heavy firs leaning low, their drooping branches brushing the top of the car with a faint swish of sound. Ahead, a blinding wall of white particles slanted down, viewed through the small segment of windscreen that the wipers reluctantly left clear.

Then Linzi saw squares of brightness pattern the dark night and knew their journey was finally at an end.

The car stopped, sliding slightly sideways, and light streamed out from the open front door to reveal a flight of partly-swept steps.

Once inside the house a clamour of excited

voices welcomed them and Linzi lost count of the number of people milling round. There seemed to be dozens, but she decided it could only be because they were all moving so quickly.

'It's getting late, Morwenna. I'll take Jonathan upstairs and give him a bath and his supper if that's OK with you,' she whispered through the hubbub. 'Where do I go?'

The baby struggled in her arms, grizzling wearily, pushing out protesting hands at the strange faces that loomed, wanting to kiss and cuddle him.

'Poor little chap,' came a brisk voice. 'Come along, I'll take you both up.'

Mrs Breage, Gavin's mother, appeared from the group, reed-thin and silver-haired, one slender hand catching Linzi's elbow to propel her forward. With a smile of relief, she followed the upright figure up a sharply-angled flight of polished wooden stairs and along a white-walled corridor.

'I've put you in what was originally the nursery wing, my dear,' Mrs Breage said, opening a door. 'It's all been redone since the fire and we've had a bathroom added. Let me know if there's anything you need, won't you? What about Jonathan's supper?' She smoothed the tips of her fingers over the baby's silky hair and kissed it gently. 'It must have been such a long journey for him, poor little scrap.'

12

'He'll be fine once he's settled down,' Linzi assured her, unwrapping Jonathan from the fleecy blanket she'd swathed round him for the short, but chilly, distance into the house. 'It's way past his usual bedtime, so I'll feed him up here, as soon as I've bathed him.'

Balancing the baby on one hip, she unzipped a hold-all and produced some small glass jars. 'These will need warming up, I'm afraid.'

'Let me have them then, my dear.'

Linzi had just finished drying Jonathan and put him into his night-clothes, when there was a knock at the door. Crooking the baby in one arm, she opened it, raising her eyes in surprise to meet those of the tall, denim-clad man who filled the doorway.

'One beef and vegetable broth and what appears to be banana custard,' he said solemnly, holding out a small tray.

'I hope it's not all you're going to have for your dinner.'

He stepped farther into the room. 'Where would you like this?' he asked, glancing round for a suitable place while the tray tilted slightly. 'My name's Alex, by the way.'

'Here, please,' she said, indicating a little table beside a low chair. 'Thanks.'

She settled herself into the cushions, and for a moment Alex stood, his dark head bent, watching as she began to spoon the food into Jonathan's eager mouth. Then, with a sudden

13

movement, he swung round and, without a word, strode to the door.

Linzi looked up, startled by the abruptness of his leaving, and was shocked by the expression on his gaunt, but good-looking face. It was one she had never seen before in a man's eyes.

They were deep pools of anguish.

CHAPTER TWO

The lounge, when Linzi found it after Jonathan was safely asleep, was vast. As Morwenna had said, a log fire was blazing in a wide granite-stone grate, surrounded by a high metal-mesh guard. Two dogs lay stretched in front of it, basking in the fierce heat, hind legs occasionally twitching.

At the far end a collection of children kneeled on the wooden parquet floor, noisily playing a game of tiddly-winks supervised, without much enthusiasm Linzi noticed, by a thin teenage girl. So thin and wan that Linzi felt sure she must be anorexic.

A small, tousle-haired boy—Linzi decided it could only be the five-year-old that Morwenna had spoken of—kept picking up his counters and deliberately dropping them into the pot, which caused roars of annoyance.

The room, with a ceiling-high Christmas tree standing against one wall, seemed overfilled, both with furniture and people, yet still remained a comfortable setting with its mingled scents of pine and wood-smoke.

When Linzi entered there was a sudden silence and everyone looked up. She was grateful when Gavin called to her from one of the deep, chintz-covered sofas to come and

15

join him.

'This is Linzi,' he said, slipping an arm round her shoulders. 'The second lady in my life.' And he slipped his other arm round his wife as he spoke, giving her an affectionate hug.

One by one, he introduced his family by name—Claire and Eve, his sisters; Philip and Guy, their husbands, seven, or maybe eight children—leaving Linzi totally bewildered as to who was who. The only name she remembered was that of Alex, leaning, long-limbed, against a corner of the ornate stone mantelpiece. regarding her with deep, troubled, blue eyes.

When they went in to dinner, Alex sat at the far end of the table talking to the thin teenager, who was Claire's eldest step-daughter, Sophie, and Linzi was able to study him without him being aware of her curiosity.

He had the same dark hair as Gavin—all the family had it—but whereas Gavin's was cut very short to quell its tendency to curl, Alex's grew thick to brush the collar of his blue, check shirt.

His face was more angular than Gavin's, the nose shorter and more defined, the jaw slightly thrusting, and when he smiled—which was a rare occurrence—she noticed a deep cleft, too straight to be mistaken for just a dimple, appear in one cheek.

And yet, despite being the youngest, he

16

looked far older than Gavin and his sisters. A furrow cut sharply between his brows into his forehead, and the lines that radiated round his mouth were not from laughter.

Linzi couldn't forget that terrible, haunted expression she'd seen earlier when he looked at Jonathan. It both puzzled and distressed her.

As she finished, her soup bowl was whisked away by a discreet hand and she turned to smile at a plump young girl whom she guessed must be one of the hotel staff kept on to help out at Christmas.

'Mind your fingers on this plate,' the girl whispered as she placed it in front of her. 'It's very hot.'

Linzi regarded the thin, slightly under-done slices of roast beef with eager anticipation—lunch on the journey seemed an age ago—and began to spoon potatoes from the dish handed to her by Claire. Then, as she went to pass it across the table to Morwenna, she stopped, the heavy dish wavering in her hand. Morwenna's eyes were fixed on Alex, and they brimmed with unshed tears.

But why? Linzi asked herself. Why should anyone reveal such infinite sadness because of Alex? And why Morwenna?

A thought hovered at the edge of her mind and she pushed it away, only to find it force its way back again as she looked at the handsome face. The thick, dark thatch of hair was swept back, hiding his strong neck; the long, tanned fingers smoothing out the starched whiteness of his serviette; his casual way of dressing—jeans and check shirt, even at so formal a meal.

On the opposite side of the table sat Gavin, immaculate in a charcoal-grey suit, blue-striped tie neatly-knotted under the collar of his white shirt, chin smooth and freshly shaved.

Gavin was a lot older than Morwenna—ten years at least. Alex and Morwenna were around the same age. Could there—had there . . .?

Linzi made herself concentrate on the food, but unwillingly her eyes kept returning to the two brothers, comparing them.

I'm being unfair, she reasoned. Morwenna and Gavin are so very much in love. Living with them as closely as she did, Linzi was only too aware of it. They couldn't be living a lie.

She remembered again that anguished expression on Alex's face. Why should his brother's son produce such a look? His brother's son.

Or, could it be that . . .? Linzi compelled herself not to let the idea crystallise in her mind, but it was impossible. It refused to be suppressed.

Could it be that Jonathan was not Gavin's child, but Alex's?

When the meal came to an end, the younger children couldn't wait to go to bed, their voices shrilling with excitement as they scampered up the long staircase, clutching the red-edged net stockings their Grandma had given them. All, Linzi noticed, except Sophie who hovered close to Alex, gazing up at him from under her thick lashes.

Remembering the way she'd seen Morwenna look at him, the thought crossed Linzi's mind that perhaps Alex was used to young women falling in love with him—and she was instantly annoyed by her own spitefulness. But then, he is an extremely handsome man, she reasoned.

As if sensing her thoughts, Alex's gaze met hers from across the lounge, and as he did, once again she saw bleak despair in his eyes.

'So what are your plans for us this year, Mother?' Claire enquired, refilling her cup from the heavy silver coffee-pot on a round table beside her chair. 'I notice you've hidden away all the television sets again.'

'Of course, dear,' her mother replied firmly. 'You know I like us to have a traditional Christmas. And this year, with snow, it will be absolutely perfect.' She paused until her daughter had put down the ornate pot. 'I want our Christmases here to be something the children will always remember when they're grown up. It's become far too commercialised for my liking. How on earth can youngsters be expected to know the true meaning of the occasion?' She lowered her silvery head as she poured cream into her coffee. 'There's no need for any of them to sit in front of a television screen all day either. We shall make our own entertainment as we always have.'

The room echoed with a series of groans.

'But, Gran,' Sophie protested, 'there are some fantastic films on telly on Christmas Day. It's not fair—you always make us miss them. I shall have nothing to talk about to the others when I go back to school.' She gave a petulant little shrug of her shoulders and headed for the door. 'I wish Mummy hadn't gone skiing in Austria or I could've asked her to video them. Now it'll have to be my friend, Kate—and she'll think I'm staying at the North Pole or somewhere just as remote and uncivilised.'

'So what is this year's plan, Mother?' Gavin enquired mildly in the empty silence that followed his niece's outburst.

'Tonight it's charades and tomorrow, being Christmas Day, there's a treasure hunt over the whole house.' Mrs Breage stopped, waiting for everyone's attention before she continued. 'And then on Boxing Day we're having a ball.'

'A ball?' Gavin echoed hollowly.

'A formal dance—not one of those dreadful disco things with flashing lights and blaring music that everyone seems to have nowadays,' his mother replied. 'I've sent out dozens of invitations. You see, while the nursery wing was being rebuilt, I had to close the hotel and restaurant for a couple of months. There was such a lot of upheaval and I really couldn't

20

expect guests to put up with that. After all, they do come here for peace and quiet.' She started to gather the empty coffee cups and pile them on the tray. 'Of course, once something like that happens, it takes a while for trade to pick up again, so I decided this would be a good way to create publicity.'

'Let me take that tray for you, Mother,' Eve said, moving forward.

Mrs Breage quelled her daughter with a frown. 'I'm not in my dotage yet, dear,' she retorted, giving the door a push with her elbow, then halted. 'You'll never guess what we found when turning out the attics a month or so back—trunks full of the most beautiful old clothes. They must have been there for centuries.' She smiled at her assembled family from the open doorway before stepping out into the corridor. 'I'm sure you'll all be able to find something amongst them to wear for the ball, so there'll be no excuses.' Her voice floated back to them. 'I did tell you it was fancy-dress, didn't I?'

*   *   *

To her surprise, Linzi enjoyed the evening's charades, despite having to run upstairs every so often to check Jonathan. All the members of the Breage family knew each other so well that none of them felt embarrassed by acting the fool, and everyone ended up convulsed

21

with laughter.

Except Alex, she noticed, who stayed remote from it all sitting on the long, red-leather window-seat at the end of the lounge, sitting feet up, denim-clad knees drawn under his chin, reading a book. It was as if he were in a world of his own, quite oblivious to the hilarity and noise surrounding him.

What seemed even more strange to her was that no-one—not even his mother—made any attempt to try to draw him into the fun. Maybe he's always been the odd one out and they're used to it by now, she mused.

But in a lull while everyone was waiting for Philip to think up an appropriate charade to illustrate his word, Linzi saw Morwenna leave the group and settle on the window-seat close beside Alex.

She remained there, talking softly to him, their heads almost touching, for the rest of the evening.

It was almost midnight when Mrs Breage insisted it was time for bed.

'There are the children's stockings to be filled,' she observed, giving their parents a frosty look. 'If you don't hurry up, they'll all be awake before you even start. And I expect every one of you down to breakfast by eight-thirty. We don't want the whole day wasted because of lie-abeds.'

It had been a tiring day, with its long journey from London to Cornwall and, after making sure that Jonathan was safely tucked up for the night, Linzi had fallen straight to sleep—until that strange cry woke her.

Now, she lay, wide awake. Taut. Listening. And yet she knew it hadn't been Jonathan who cried.

Outside, there was an eerie light. A sort of brilliance. Snow at night has that effect, she recalled, slipping out of bed to stand by the window and look down in the garden. In the moonlight it was magical, every tree silhouetted against the dark sky by its white branches.

Faintly, in the distance, she could hear the soft surge of waves and wondered what it would be like to be there on the beach, stepping on snow instead of sand. For one impulsive moment she was tempted to slip on her clothes again and find out. But then she remembered Jonathan. There was no way she could leave him. If he woke . . . and in an unfamiliar room, too . . .

The moon was hidden behind a wisp of cloud, leaving only the reflection of the snow to reveal the expanse of garden like some giant Christmas card. With a twist of excitement spiralling through her, Linzi realised it was Christmas Day. A day that would be so very different from those she'd spent previously. In recent years there'd been just the two of them—her great-aunt and herself, after her parents were killed.

23

A shudder radiated down her spine. Even now, in the safety of the room, with four thick walls surrounding her, she could still visualise shattering particles of glass glitter like diamonds in the motorway lights; hear the unbelievable rend and grind of metal; feel the impact that sent her hurtling from the rear seat, through the door as it burst outwards, on to the roadside.

And then, nothing. Only a suffocating heaviness that vibrated with the echo of sirens, voices; hollow sounds in a black void.

Her great-aunt had been kind, but over-protective. I was all she had left, Linzi thought. What else could she be? She was far too old to have, suddenly, to cope with a young child. And money wasn't easy. Her parents had enjoyed life. Saving is something to do in the future, when we're middle-aged, not now, they'd always said. And as for insurance . . .

It must have been difficult for Aunt Margaret, Linzi thought sadly.

Somewhere, out in the garden, an owl hooted, making her shiver. Was that what woke me? she wondered. An owl? And yet, somehow she felt sure it had been a baby's cry. Perhaps one of the staff has a child? Tomorrow, she decided with a yawn, I'll find out.

Breakfast was a haphazard affair. Despite Mrs Breage's order of eight-thirty, everyone seemed to come and go as they pleased. The

24

children were dancing around in a frenzy, waving the small presents they'd discovered in their stockings, and growing more impatient with every minute to open the gifts piled under the Christmas tree in the lounge.

'Not until after lunch,' their grandmother instructed in a decisive tone. 'And no squeezing or shaking the parcels either. Marcus, make quite sure you remember that. We don't want a repeat of last year, do we, when we spent half the day picking up bits of that ghetto-blaster your parents so mistakenly gave you? Morning service is at eleven and I expect all of you to attend. We shall walk down at half past ten.' Her head turned. 'And please dress in something more suitable, Alexander. Go up and change this instant,' she said sternly, eyeing the jeans her younger son wore.

Then her shrewd gaze moved to Linzi who was trying to spoon cereal into Jonathan's reluctant mouth, as his eyes followed the movements of his lively cousins.

'Babies are especially welcome at the Christmas service, my dear. And round this way they are few and far between.'

'So you can't escape either,' Alex murmured, bending to speak as he passed her chair.

'I just hope he doesn't cry. All this upheaval's a bit unsettling for him,' Linzi said anxiously, and then remembering the previous night, asked, 'By the way, is there another baby

25

in the house? I'm sure I heard one in the night—and it wasn't Jonathan. He was fast asleep. Exhausted by all that travelling.'

Alex's tall frame stiffened. 'You probably dreamed it,' he said, and his voice was terse. 'Or maybe it was an owl. We get quite a few of them in the grounds at this time of year.'

Linzi shook her head as she wiped away a spoonful of cereal that had missed its destination. 'No. It was a baby. Much younger than Jonathan, too, from the sound of it.'

And when she looked up at him, she was disturbed to see Alex's expression draw once more into deep lines of pain, before he swiftly headed away and out into the corridor.

As she reached the stairs to prepare Jonathan for his outing, Mrs Breage caught up with her. 'There's a splendid old pram in the utility room beside the kitchen, my dear,' she said. 'I had it for all my children. You won't need to use that flimsy little buggy thing. Jonathan will be far warmer in it, and there's a hood if it comes on to snow again. With its large wheels, you'll probably find it far easier to push.'

And Linzi knew better than to dispute the fact with her.

CHAPTER THREE

The procession that set out for church later that morning was a strangely assorted group, well wrapped up against the cold in thick scarves, hats and heavy tweed coats.

Mrs Breage led the way down the winding lane at a fast pace, with Claire and Philip's collection of children darting and leaping around her. Linzi still wasn't quite sure exactly how many there were.

Eve's wayward five-year-old, Marcus, loudly protesting, was held firmly in his grandmother's grip while he half-ran to keep up with her.

Then, more slowly, came the adults, catching up on family news, their breath spiralling white clouds in the cold air as they chatted animatedly together.

Behind them, Linzi struggled with the enormous high-wheeled old pram. Well-wrapped in a fringed, check blanket, Jonathan sat in splendour, straining against the leather harness as he tried to lean out from under the hood and peer over the sides at the new world passing by.

The snow in the lane was deep where it had drifted, piled like crisp meringue, their footprints marring its perfection. Every few yards or so the pram wheels came to a jolting halt when they became coated with frozen lumps.

Linzi noticed that Alex hadn't joined the party. At least one of the family is strong enough to rebel against their mother, she thought, until a strong tanned hand appeared beside hers on the pram handle, aiding its propulsion as the wheels clogged yet again.

When she turned her head to look at him, to her surprise the well-worn jeans were gone, replaced by a sheepskin jacket below which immaculately pressed charcoal-grey trouser-legs appeared, and were lost in a pair of rather muddy, green wellies.

As if reading her thoughts, he gave a wry smile. 'Well, my mother can't expect total perfection in weather like this, can she?' he enquired drily.

The baby bent forward to pat a passing snowflake with one mittened hand, the white bobble on his woollen hat flopping sideways. Linzi gently eased him back under the pram hood and tucked the blanket more closely around him. When she looked back at Alex again, his mouth was a tight narrow line.

'He's beautiful,' Linzi said. 'But then I'm biased.'

Alex lightly smoothed the baby's plump cheek with one finger, and it was seized by two fat fists and swiftly steered towards a waiting mouth.

'No, Jonathan,' she warned.

The baby gazed back at her with huge, reproachful blue eyes and let the finger escape again.

'Don't you sometimes wish he were your own child?' Alex asked her. 'You're with him all day, every day. Surely you must resent it a little when you see Morwenna with him?'

Linzi shook her head. 'Of course not,' she replied with a smile. 'We both love him. Equally, but in different ways. Morwenna is his mother. I could never replace that kind of love. And Jonathan must benefit, mustn't he? Being loved so much can only be a good thing. For anyone,' she added softly, steering the pram round a branch weighed down by snow that blocked their path.

Alex made no answer and they continued walking, following the footprints of the rest of the party who were striding on rapidly, well ahead now. Linzi could hear the sound of their voices, but not their words.

'Your mother mentioned that the house has been closed as a hotel for rebuilding to be carried out to the nursery wing,' she said. 'What happened?'

Alex's voice was flat, almost toneless when he replied. 'There was a fire. A child . . . and its mother . . . were suffocated by the smoke.'

Linzi stared back at him, horrified, seeing the tortured expression return to his eyes once more, turning their blue to a desolate grey.

'How simply terrible,' she breathed,

horrified by his terse statement.

'It was.'

His voice tailed away, and for a moment, as she watched a myriad of emotions flit across his face, Linzi felt sure he was about to say more, but then his mother called from farther on down the lane.

'Do hurry up, Alexander. The five-minute bell has started. With so many of us, it will look dreadful if we walk in late.'

Their conversation ceased as Alex put his strength behind the reluctant pram and they hurried over the snow to catch up.

* * *

The church was small and sturdy, its tower square with pinnacles like a castle from which the bells rang out clearly in the cold air. Swept snow lay in melting heaps at the side of the narrow path as they went through the rusting wrought-iron gate.

Linzi bumped the pram down the worn stone step of the porch and through the low-arched wooden door, then seated herself at the back with it in the aisle beside her. The rest of the family didn't appear to notice as they made their way ahead to squash into three of the front pews. But as she kneeled on a fraying hassock, Linzi heard a movement beside her and when she rose again, found that Alex had joined her, his head already bent in prayer.

The inside of the church was beautiful. Huge swathes of holly and fir decorated every round stone pillar, while bowls of chrysanthemums, intermingled with pale haloes of honesty, glowed on the windowsills. The only light came from candles, flickering on either side, stirred by a draught from the open door.

Linzi couldn't believe the sense of peace. Centuries of prayer, suspended in time, surrounded her like a balm. For once even Alex's taut face was calm.

She pushed back the hood of the pram and watched the baby's enrapt expression as he gazed round with blue eyes. Linzi looked sideways at the tall man beside her. Is Jonathan his child? she wondered. Was that the reason for the torment so apparent on his face whenever he was near him?

Gavin is a great deal older than his wife, and Alex is incredibly like his brother—had that drawn Morwenna to him? She asked herself. But would Morwenna then have been so willing to come and stay here for Christmas?

And would Alex—knowing that the child would be there, too?

Or perhaps he was curious? A man would want to see his son, wouldn't he?

But then, when he did . . .

Did that explain Alex's haunted expression?

Linzi tried hard to dismiss the thoughts; to

concentrate on the service. Rising to her feet to sing, her hand rested next to Alex's on the page of the hymnbook they shared, almost touching. And when she glanced up, it was to find his steady gaze on her, not the words.

It startled her, and for the rest of the service her concentration was lost, while her heartbeat seemed to echo in her ears in a strangely uneven way.

The long oak table was magnificent when they all went in to eat. Silver and crystal gleamed against the polished wood; scarlet serviettes and crackers glowed beside each setting, and elaborate arrangements of greenery and baubles were placed at intervals down the centre.

It was a Christmas lunch such as Linzi had never experienced before. First came a clear soup, then thin slivers of fish in a delicious creamy sauce, followed by a sharp lemon sorbet to clear the palate before the largest turkey she had even seen was wheeled in with a side of beef and joint of pork. The Christmas pudding blazed in brandy-fed flames, to be eaten with thick clusters of clotted cream. After that Linzi gave up, reluctantly refusing a variety of cheeses and biscuits, and tempting selection of fruit and chocolate mints.

With a different wine served with each course, she felt blissful and contented, but even so couldn't prevent herself from watching Morwenna, trying to detect some sign, some hint, of her relationship with Alex who sat next to her. But they appeared quite casual together. No lingering glances. No surreptitious touches. Nothing.

Maybe it's over, Linzi decided. Or never was.

Afterwards, everyone took their coffee into the lounge, then the present opening began with paper and children flying everywhere. Despite a wealth of toys that Linzi and Morwenna helped him unwrap, Jonathan was far more interested in gathering up every coloured scrap to cram into an empty box, and then take out again, repeatedly.

As the afternoon wore on, the adults began to doze, heads lolling against the back of their chairs. Every so often a faint snore would quiver forth, creating a riot of giggles from the children who'd settled down to play with their new toys.

A soporific hush descended, to be violently broken when Marcus discovered Jonathan's box of paper and leaned over the guard to tip the contents into the fire, sending a blaze of flames roaring up the chimney.

For a few seconds, there was panic as charred and smouldering fragments floated above the grate, before sinking gradually down again.

'He'll probably grow up to be an arsonist—or maybe a fireman,' Morwenna murmured to Linzi once the scare was over. 'Or more likely

33

a delinquent, in years to come.'

But Linzi wasn't listening. Her attention was drawn to Alex, who was sitting as if carved from stone, the bones of his face showing white through the tan of his skin, while his eyes stared in horror at the leaping flames.

Noting her silence, Morwenna followed the direction of her gaze, then rose swiftly to kneel beside him, one hand reaching out to close over his, her head hiding his tortured face from Linzi's view.

Jonathan had fallen asleep on the floor in a cocoon of crumpled paper, thumb tucked in his mouth, and Linzi bent to lift him onto her lap. At the movement, Morwenna twisted round and took the baby from her.

'It's Christmas Day, Lin.' She smiled, but her eyes were swimming with tears as she lowered her head to kiss the baby's silky hair. 'Take a while off. I'll keep an eye on Jonathan. He'll sleep for hours anyway.'

'I could do with some air,' Linzi confessed, with a wide yawn. 'Any minute now I shall nod off like the others. Perhaps I'll go for a walk in the garden.'

'Well, wrap up warm,' Morwenna advised. 'There's a bitter wind out there. You'll find some wellies in the little room next to the kitchen door. Dozens of pairs have been gathered there over the years as everyone's grown up. One pair is sure to fit you.'

Under its blanket of snow, the lawn was

smooth, marred only by a faint etching of threadlike footprints left by the birds. Linzi was reluctant to spoil such perfection. Somewhere there must be a path.

Carefully she stepped forward, her feet in their borrowed wellingtons sinking deep. There was a weird, almost ethereal silence. Only the sea pounding in the distance made any sound. Linzi decided to find it.

To the right of the house the ground dropped steeply between tall pines and bare oaks. It had to be a path. She trudged on, the boots slipping slightly on her feet with every step she took.

Even though the snow had stopped falling, the sky still had the look of tarnished pewter, heavy and dull, so that for a while she didn't realise that the view glimpsed through gaps in the trees was the sea. Its slate colour merged into that above with no clear division.

And then, without any warning, came a flint stone wall, waist-high, with a gap in the middle. Linzi guessed there must be steps leading down. Probing with one cautious toe, she found the first, then the next, until finally she stood on what she could only imagine was a bank of shingle.

Ahead, waves curled silently inwards, meeting the snow, revealing the pale gold of fine sand beyond its edge. The unexpected sight delighted her.

Around her, high, flat, sloping shelves of

granite stretched out from the woods to create a secluded and sheltered cove. Eagerly she stepped forward, the salty smell of seaweed catching at her throat, feeling the slight shift of shingle far below her feet, until she stood at the very edge of the shore, letting the water surge round her boots.

Through the swirling depths she could see tiny stones, jewel-bright; thin, delicate wisps of feathery weed that drifted to and fro with the movement of each wave; a crab's claw swaying in the eddy.

Caught among the rocks were small pools, edged with pale fronds. Within them tiny creatures darted and scurried. Linzi leaned forward, resting her gloved hands on the limpet-covered granite, her fair hair falling forward round her cheeks. Impatiently, she tucked it back into the hood of her anorak.

'It's amazing that minute little things like that can survive such freezing water, when you or I would be dead within minutes.' A quiet voice spoke and Linzi spun round, her feet sliding on the shingle beneath the snow, to be caught in Alex's strong grip. 'Sorry, Lin! I didn't mean to startle you.'

Linzi's sigh of relief misted in the air, and she smiled ruefully at him.

'I thought I was completely alone,' she confided in him. 'It's like another world, down here.'

Alex nodded, perching himself on a ledge of

36

rock and staring out to where tree branches reached down into the water a distance away.

'It is another world,' he agreed. 'That's the mouth of the Helford river, with the open sea ahead,' he said, pointing across the water. 'Quite a contrast to those secluded reaches. We had the best of both worlds as children.'

'And now?' she asked. 'Where do you live?'

He turned his head and she saw the wind lift his dark hair raggedly over his forehead, hiding the deep furrow marring it, so that in the growing twilight he looked like a boy again.

'Still here,' he replied. 'I manage the hotel now for my mother.' A faint smile caught at the corners of his wide mouth. 'Once, you see, I trained to be an accountant. It came in useful in the end.'

'You don't look like an accountant,' Linzi said. 'I mean . . . well, they're usually . . . well . . .' She stopped.

'Neat and tidy?' he enquired with a quizzical life of his eyebrows.

'Sometimes,' she agreed weakly.

His long fingers picked up a thin flake of shale and deftly skimmed it across the tip of the waves. Linzi saw it bounce once, twice, three times, before it vanished.

'Perhaps that's why I gave up. Neatness and tidiness aren't quite me somehow.'

From among the rocks a grey, long-legged bird appeared, strutting stiffly along the

37

shallows, striped head poised, beak held ready.

'A heron,' Alex breathed, bending closer for her to hear and a strand of his hair brushed her forehead sending a quiver of sensation pulsing through her. 'They're usually over by the river-bank but maybe this one's hungry.'

She saw the beady yellow of its eye search the depths, then the narrow beak dip and lift, twisting sideways before its skinny neck convulsed as the bird swallowed.

'Not lavish for a Christmas dinner,' Alex observed with a chuckle, and at the sound the heron rose in the air and flapped heavily away turning inland towards the far bank of the river.

'They nest in the trees over there.'

'I imagined they were like swans,' Linzi said, 'and nested on the ground, being so big.'

Alex shook his head. 'No. If I had my binoculars here, I could show you. You probably can't see from this distance and in this light but the heronry is halfway along there.' He placed his hand on her shoulder to turn her in the right direction and her breath faltered at the touch. 'And just beyond that is where the cormorants roost. You can tell from the branches and rocks below. They're almost white. We get a number of different birds along the Helford. You must come here again in the spring. I often take the boat up Frenchman's Creek. It's beautiful, with the newly-green trees dipping right down into the water. Quite breath-taking.' His blue eyes studied her thoughtfully. 'I think you'd like it, too.'

'You sail?' she said.

He smiled, making the lines of tension round his mouth vanish. 'We all do. It's a must, living here. There are so many places along the creeks you could never find without a boat.'

A flurry of wind blew in across the sea, bringing the sharp sting of snow and Linzi watched flakes settle on the darkness of his hair.

'Maybe we should start back,' he said, turning up the sheepskin collar of his jacket. 'It'll be dark soon.'

She hadn't noticed the growing dusk, but now she saw one lone star wink from the depths of cloud, then vanish again.

'I'm sure you'd hate to miss the treasure hunt,' he added with a glimmer of wry humour. 'Careful, these steps are treacherous, even without the snow. Here, give me your hand.'

Linzi felt the strength of his fingers close round hers, and it wasn't until they reached the garden again that she realised her hand was still clasped in his and, with regret, quickly disentangled it.

The rest of the family were just starting tea when they arrived in the lounge. Two trolleys had been wheeled in, laden with doily-covered plates of tiny sandwiches, biscuits and a multitude of cakes.

Linzi, her cheeks glowing as she met the heat of the room, filled her plate and went to find an empty chair, seeing Alex sink down on his heels beside Marcus, who was munching his way through a mince pie.

'Not more food, young man!' Alex groaned. 'Where do you put it all?'

The little boy regarded him with serious eyes and patted his tummy.

'In here,' he said solemnly. 'All people do. We learned about it at my school. It goes round and round all funny tangled-up tubes. Mrs Thorley, my teacher, showed us on a picture. It was all coloured and the food had little blue arrow-things to show it the way round.' He gave a wicked chuckle, then with a wary glance at his mother lowered his voice to a hoarse whisper. 'Do you know where it comes out, Uncle Alex?'

Hiding a smile, Alex rose to his feet. 'I can guess, Marcus. There's no need to tell me.'

With a wicked giggle, the child stuffed in the last bit of crumbly pastry and crowed loudly, 'And that's where this mince pie's going, too.'

Linzi discovered the walk to the sea had revived her appetite and was soon enjoying cucumber sandwiches, followed by a large slice of fruity tea-cake, while she quenched her thirst with fragrant Earl Grey tea from a wafer-thin, flowered, china cup.

Across the room, where Alex balanced his long frame on the arm of a sofa, she saw Sophie curl herself into the gap left between him and Morwenna, who was already seated there.

Despite the wide choice of delicacies, the girl was not eating, and Linzi noticed that Alex tried to tempt her with food from his own plate.

Is she anorexic? Linzi wondered. Sophie hadn't appeared at breakfast, and at lunch she had pushed a slice of turkey round her plate, and then left it hidden amongst a pile of uneaten vegetables.

Frequently girls of that age were thin, but Sophie was particularly stick-like, with bones jutting from every angle of her body. Even her waist-length hair appeared colourless as it drifted in a fine mist around her. She seemed like a forlorn, lost soul; too old to be a child, yet too young to be grown-up.

A desolate age, Linzi recalled. Perhaps that's why she stays so close to Alex, empathising with his sadness.

Mrs Breage was in a deep armchair, with Jonathan cuddled sleepily in her lap, still clutching one of his precious scraps of wrapping paper.

When Linzi came to gather him up ready for bed, she smiled contentedly and said, 'Don't worry about that, my dear. You join in the treasure hunt. I set the clues, so there's no way I can take part. Besides, my grandson and I need to get to know each other again. It's months since I last saw him.'

'Are you quite sure?' Linzi enquired. 'I'm not really supposed to be on holiday, you know.'

'Everyone should be on holiday on Christmas Day, my dear,' Mrs Breage replied firmly, hugging her grandson more closely. 'And this, for me, is what being on holiday is all about. Off you go and enjoy yourself and forget about Jonathan. I'll take good care of him, don't you worry.'

The treasure hunt was a riotous affair, with shrieking children appearing and disappearing in every room. Linzi hadn't realised the house was quite so large, until she found herself lost several times in it.

One clue, she felt sure, led to the attics and it wasn't until she had climbed a narrow flight of stairs that she heard the quiet murmur of a voice ahead of her.

Morwenna's voice.

'You must try to forget, Alex. Please don't go on feeling so bitter. You will find someone else, one day, whom you'll love just as much.' The voice lowered and Linzi could only just catch the words that followed. 'And have another child.'

Hastily, Linzi flew down the attic stairs on silent feet, not wanting to listen to Alex reply.

CHAPTER FOUR

So Jonathan is Alex's child, Linzi thought. How terrible it must be for him, to have the baby here for Christmas. No wonder he looks so strained at times. But then, why stay? Surely a handsome man like Alex could spend his Christmas anywhere—with anyone.

For Linzi now, the treasure hunt was over. Dejectedly, she hurried along the corridor to the nursery where she found Jonathan and his grandmother engaged in a game of 'This little piggy went to market', with his toes.

'This takes me back years to when Gavin was small,' Mrs Breage declared happily. 'Although I'm afraid once Alexander came along, what with the girls as well, I didn't have a spare moment for playing games any more.' She kissed the top of Jonathan's head. 'Never mind, I'm making up for it now, aren't I, my lovely little man?'

'I think it's time he went to bed,' Linzi suggested. 'After such an exciting day, he'll fall asleep in minutes.'

'Can I help you bath him?' a plaintive voice asked and Linzi looked round to see young Marcus hovering in the doorway.

'What about the treasure hunt?' she said, hoping to deter him.

'Oh, I've found the treasure,' he replied

43

disarmingly. 'I saw Grandma hide it and went there first. Look.' He held out the remains of a box of chocolates from behind his back.

'Oh, *Marcus!*' Mrs Breage scolded. 'You little monkey!'

'*Can* I help bath Jonathan?' he pleaded, ignoring her and concentrating his attention on Linzi. 'I want to see if babies float like boats do. We did all about boats at school. My teacher took us on a river and we went on a gigantic, great big boat with an upstairs. It had all wooden seats and three of us had to sit on one together. And even with all those people, it floated. Babies are quite small, so they should float ever so easily.'

'Somehow,' Mrs Breage observed, giving Linzi a faint smile, 'I think it would be wise if I stayed to help as well.'

*   *   *

Around nine o'clock several neighbours and friends of the family came for drinks and later, feeling rather out of their conversation, Linzi decided to go to bed and read the book on Mozart that Andrew had given her as a present.

Andrew. With a guilty start, she realised she'd forgotten all about him, meaning to phone earlier and wish him a happy Christmas. Linzi glanced at her watch. It was far too late now.

After she'd showered and climbed into bed, her mind started to run back over the events of the day. But somehow, no matter how hard she tried to think of other things, her thoughts kept returning to the secluded little beach—and to Alex—recalling every word he'd spoken.

Her eyelids grew heavy. It had been a wonderful day. Possibly the nicest Christmas she'd ever had. With a sigh of contentment, she snuggled down into the softness of the covers and drifted dreamily to sleep.

The cry startled her into wakefulness again. The same thin, pathetic wail—and with a shiver of apprehension she recalled what Alex had told her about the nursery wing.

There'd been a fire—and a child and its mother had suffocated.

From the adjoining room came the rattle of the cot moving—and something more—a faint creak like the rocking of a cradle. Wide awake now, Linzi tugged on her dressing-gown and hurried in.

Jonathan was standing on the pillow at one end, moonlight outlining his pale hair like a halo. One small finger pointed as he beamed at her, revealing pearly little teeth.

'Ba-bee.'

Every day he was acquiring a vocabulary of new words, but this was one he'd never tried before.

Linzi slowly turned her head, following the

direction of his gaze to one shadowed end of the room.

'Ba-bee,' Jonathan repeated firmly.

For one fleeting second, Linzi saw the pale outline of a child, and then she heard that long-drawn-out trail of sound waver through the air again.

Her terrified scream brought Morwenna running into the room, followed by the tousled figure of Gavin.

'Lin! What's wrong?' she cried. 'Is Jonathan all right?'

The harsh brightness of the light dazzled Linzi's eyes, making her close them tightly for a second, and when she opened them it was to stare into the empty corner of the room, where all the shadows were now gone.

'I thought . . . I heard . . .' she stammered.

Morwenna threw her an anxious look as she tucked Jonathan down into the covers. 'What frightened you?'

Linzi pushed back her hair with a despairing gesture. 'I don't know,' she said. 'I'm sure there was a baby crying. It woke me.' Her gaze turned to Jonathan, already curled into sleep. 'I thought it was Jonathan.'

'He's fine, Lin,' Morwenna assured her, bending over the cot to stroke her sleeping son's head.

Gavin gave Linzi a comforting grin. 'Too much Christmas pudding and brandy sauce giving you nightmares, that's what it is.'

'But I wasn't dreaming,' Linzi protested. 'And I could hear a sound . . . a sort of creaking . . .' She stared round the room, searching for some kind of explanation.

'I expect it was the cot,' Gavin declared. 'Jonathan, feeling bored, gave it a good shake to attract some attention.'

'He kept saying "Baby".'

'New word for him,' Gavin suggested. 'So I dare say he was making quite sure you didn't miss it.'

'But he pointed . . . over there . . .' she blurted out.

'There's a mirror on the dressing table, Lin. He saw himself in that.'

'It was dark, Gavin,' she insisted.

'But wasn't the night-light turned on?' Morwenna asked. 'You usually do that, Lin, when he's sleeping.'

'Yes,' Linzi admitted reluctantly. 'Even so, it wasn't enough to see anything. And I did hear that cry.'

An owl hooted somewhere in the garden and Gavin smiled reassuringly at her, nodding his head towards the window. 'There you are, Lin. That explains what you heard. Nothing to panic about after all.' He slipped his arm round Morwenna.

'Come on, love. Back to bed. Not that there's much of the night left, but tomorrow's going to be another hectic, action-packed day if my mother has anything to do with it.'

47

'Are you sure you're all right, Lin?' Morwenna asked. 'Would you like a hot drink or something?'

Linzi shook her head. 'No, I'm fine.'

She moved slowly towards the adjoining door leading from the nursery into her own room.

'I expect you're right,' she said, trying desperately to convince herself, too. 'It was an owl . . . and Jonathan's reflection in the mirror.'

'Sleep tight then.'

In the silence of her bedroom Linzi lay uneasily, her ears tuned for a repetition of the sounds, but all she could hear was the soft swish of the sea. It was a soothing, hypnotic sound, and finally she slept.

*   *   *

'Now, you won't forget about the dance tonight, will you?' Mrs Breage instructed her family at breakfast the following morning. 'I've had Trenowth bring down those trunks of old clothes from the attic. They're in the room next to Claire and Philip's. There's sure to be something to fit everyone. If not, then you'll find needles and cotton in the sewing-room.'

She frowned at her youngest son who was sitting at the end of the long table, finishing a slice of toast.

'And remember, Alexander, that means you

48

as well.'

'Somehow, Mother,' he replied drily, 'I don't think my attempts at needlework would be appreciated.'

'Then I'm sure Linzi will help you,' she retorted briskly. 'I want no excuses, young man. Off you go now. Any more of that toast and marmalade will only make it more difficult to find a costume to fit.'

'We'll all go,' Gavin soothed, putting down his serviette and rising to his feet. 'Then we can fight over who has what.'

'Well, I hope they're clean,' Eve grumbled as they filed out of the room and began to climb the wide staircase. 'The thought of putting on something that hasn't been worn for centuries makes my skin creep.'

'Surely not centuries?' her sister replied. 'After all, the house is only three hundred years old at the most.'

'Two hundred, three hundred, what does it matter?' Eve snapped. 'The idea still repulses me. How do we know *who's* been in them before, or even what they died of?'

When they entered the room, they found the walls already hung with garments and there were cries of excitement as everyone hurried forward to examine them.

'Oh, this is beautiful!' Morwenna enthused, lifting a long, silky dress in a deep shade of rose and holding it in front of herself.

'Very nineteen twenties,' Gavin observed,

smiling fondly at his wife. 'The colour suits you, darling. Will it fit? How about this for me?'

Linzi stood on the edge of the family group. It was their home, and she didn't like to push forward and start grabbing at the clothes as they were doing.

'We'll take the left-overs, shall we, Lin?' Alex was leaning against the doorpost behind her, head slightly bent to avoid the low lintel. 'I'm hoping to find a suit of armour.'

'Rather difficult for dancing, don't you think?' she suggested.

One of his rare smiles curved his lips, sending a crinkle of tiny lines outwards from his eyes to vanish into the thick dark hair curling over his ears.

'I could always be placed in a corner and left to observe.'

'Would you prefer that?'

He didn't answer, but stepped farther into the room and moved leisurely towards the growing heap of clothes that the rest of his family were tossing onto the four-poster bed.

'This,' he said, picking up a mist of white muslin, 'should be for you.'

'A suitable dress for a nursemaid?' she enquired doubtfully.

'No,' he replied. 'A suitable dress for a young lady attending her first ball. Haven't you noticed that painting on the stairs as you come up? Annabel Breage. The one with all the

50

golden ringlets. I should imagine she's wearing this, or something very similar, and she's around your age and colouring.'

'But she was a daughter of the family, not a nanny.'

'What does that matter?' he said, raising his dark eyebrows.

'Well . . .'

'Good gracious, Lin! We're in the twentieth century, not Victorian times. Wenna and Gavin regard you as part of the family—we all do.' He put the dress back on the bed again. 'But if you don't like it . . .'

'Oh, but I do,' Linzi said eagerly. 'It's just that . . . What about your sisters and Morwenna? Or even Sophie?'

'If you look at Claire and Eve, neither of them is sylph-like enough to fit into a dress this size, and Morwenna's already chosen hers.'

He glanced across to where the teenage Sophie was tugging an elaborate black, velvet affair over her head and skipping towards a long mirror against the wall. 'Sophie's in a black phase at the moment—as you'll have noticed from all her Christmas presents, so this certainly won't appeal.'

The others, their arms draped with clothes, were starting to return to their respective rooms.

'Well, they appear to have made their selection. Have a look through what's left, Lin,

51

to see what you prefer. I think I'll go for this dinner jacket—it looks quite presentable and totally out of keeping with me.' He delved into the pile of remaining garments. 'If you come across a suitable shirt and bow tie, fish them out for me, will you? Oh, and a pair of trousers. Jeans always seem to offend my mother in some strange way.'

Linzi chose the white muslin dress, but it needed taken in. Studying the portrait critically later, she decided Annabel had been rather more well-endowed than her, so while Jonathan had his morning nap she spent the time neatly taking in the side seams a fraction and pressing out the wrinkles.

Twisting a strand of her long fair hair round one finger, she gazed thoughtfully into the mirror of her dressing-table, and wondered whether she could create suitable ringlets. Somehow her straight, unfussy style wasn't quite right with such a dress.

Outside in the garden shrieks of laughter suddenly burst forth, and looking out Linzi saw some of the children using the steep slope of the lawn for a toboggan run, while the others made a snowman.

Sophie, she noticed, hovered on the edge of them, plainly trying to decide whether her newly-acquired teenage status permitted her to join in. Only when Alex appeared, and distributed what appeared to be a collection of silver trays from under his arm, then slid down the hill on one of them, did the girl relax and enthusiastically follow suit.

Poor scrap, Linzi reflected. Neither a child, nor a grown-up, yet wanting to be both. Those early teenage years are the worst of all. And how obviously she adores Alex.

The memory of Morwenna's sad eyes watching him across the dinner-table came back to Linzi. Maybe all women do, she mused.

An indignant rattling of his cot from the next room told her Jonathan was awake, and after changing his nappy and zipping him into his padded anorak and trousers, she tucked him into the family pram and went out into the garden.

'Come to play?' Alex teased.

Linzi smiled and shook her head.

'We've got a wooden sledge as well as these trays,' Marcus told her, running to catch hold of her hand with his snowy glove. 'You can sit on that if you like. It's not so cold for your bottom.'

'How can you refuse?' Alex murmured. 'Sophie'll keep an eye on Jonathan, won't you?'

Marcus was already tugging Linzi forward.

'I'll show you what to do. It's two at a time. You sit there. That's right. And I'll be here, in the front. Hold onto these bits of rope. They make it go the right way.'

He gave a shriek of delight as the sledge went rushing down the slope, then tipped over sideways when Linzi jerked the rope in an effort to control its rapid progress.

'Why did you stop us? Uncle Alex makes it go much farther than that. Miles and miles,' Marcus complained as they hauled it back up again. 'You show Linzi how to do it properly, Uncle Alex.'

Before she could protest, Linzi was seated at the front of the sledge, with Alex's knees firmly gripping her on either side, his arms holding the rope taut, the warmth of his breath catching her cheek as he leaned forward. The children gave a vigorous heave, and they were heading down the slope.

She felt the muscles in Alex's arms tighten around her and saw his wrists twist as the tall trunks of the pines flashed past, then the sledge was racing along the winding path.

Linzi's anorak hood blew back, releasing her hair in a wild cloud and as it obscured his vision, Alex's head bent swiftly, his cheek ice-cold against hers while he endeavoured to see. For a moment she thought the sudden movement would send them off the path and into the trees, but the sledge straightened course, its speed increasing, snow rising high to scatter around them and powder her skin.

Her breath was snatched away; she felt light-headed with exhilaration, a smile of sheer joy catching at her lips.

And then, ahead of them, she caught sight of the flint-stone wall half-buried in its mantle of snow.

They were travelling too fast to stop now and the high, snowy banks of the garden bordering the path prevented any diversion.

Petrified, she leaned backwards against Alex, closing her eyes. Instantly, she was a child again, in the car with her parents on that fatal day, hearing the screech of tyres and rend of metal, seeing the glittering shatter of glass, with its never-to-be-forgotten bottomless pit of darkness waiting to reclaim her once more.

CHAPTER FIVE

The harsh rasp of the sledge runners against the crisp surface of the snow echoed in her ears, followed by the sharp intake of Alex's breath. The roar of the sea resounded around her. Time ceased.

Linzi braced her body for the sickening impact that must come as they hurtled into the rough stone—and then opened her eyes in surprise. The sledge had come to a halt.

Alex's arms loosened their grip around her, his warmth moving away.

'That was close,' he murmured.

'We came through the gap?' she questioned, unable to believe it.

'Without even touching the sides.' There was laughter in his voice.

Chill began to seep into her and quickly she brushed away the snow that buried her feet and legs. When Alex held out a hand, she seized it gratefully, letting him pull her upright.

'I really thought we were going to smash straight into it,' she breathed, turning her head to stare at the sharp flints of the wall.

Alex bent and picked up the thin rope. 'So did I.'

'It was a brilliant bit of steering.'

'More luck than judgement, I'm afraid,' he

admitted, righting the sledge. 'Can you manage the climb back? It's going to be pretty slippery, I'm afraid. Sit on this thing if you like and I'll tow you back up the hill.'

'After that?' She laughed. 'No way!'

A babble of voices clamoured shrilly and the children appeared, slipping and slithering down the path.

'We thought you'd crashed and were dead,' Marcus shrieked, giving Linzi an enthusiastic hug, then stepped back to study her. *Did* you crash? You're all snowy.'

'Nearly,' she said, smiling at Alex, 'but not quite.'

'Gran came out just after you'd gone to say it's lunch-time and we'd better buck up or we won't get any. Sophie's taken your baby indoors so's he can have his. Are there going to be crackers again today? I had a shiny red paper fish in my one yesterday and when you put it on your hand it curls up. I'm going to take it to school when we go home and show it to my teacher.'

He kept up a constant stream of chatter, clinging to her hand as he tugged her to the top of the garden, followed by Alex and the others pulling the sledge. Once indoors, he let go and raced off towards the dining-room.

'Marcus!' Linzi called after him. 'Take off those boots first.'

'But I'm hungry,' he protested, reluctantly returning to her.

57

'Off!' she commanded. 'Where are your slippers? Your toes are like icicles.'

Marcus frowned down at his feet. 'What's icicles?'

She lifted him up and carried him over to the window. 'Up there. See? Hanging from the gutter.'

'My toes don't look all cold and spiky like that,' he declared.

'Well, they will, if you don't put on your slippers and some dry socks. These are soaking. Off you go and find them, quickly,' she said, putting him down at the foot of the stairs.

'Will you wait for me then? Please, Linzi,' he begged, looking up at her imploringly.

She glanced through the dining-room door to see that Morwenna had already settled Jonathan in his high-chair and was feeding him. 'OK, then, if you hurry.'

'And how about me, Lin?' Alex's voice came quietly from the corridor behind her. 'Will you wait for me, too?'

She spun round, but his eyes were hidden as he bent forward to pull off his own boots, and she couldn't read whether there was any teasing in their expression . . .

*   *   *

The ball was to start at eight o'clock that evening, so the younger children were hustled

58

off early to bed and the older ones left to play board games in the lounge. There was some grumbling amongst them when they found that Sophie was to be allowed to join the grown-ups, but once they knew she was on a strict time-limit of ten-thirty, their muttering ceased.

Marcus pleaded with Linzi to read him a story from *Winnie The Pooh*.

'Or else I'll have nasty thoughts about ghosts and monsters, creeping out from all those dark corners,' he wailed, 'and never go to sleep, ever again.'

So by the time she'd bathed Jonathan and given him his supper, then settled Marcus, it was well past eight and she still had to get dressed. Cars had been crunching up the drive for the past half hour, and the rise and fall of voices rose up to her from the hall.

Swiftly she had to make do with twisting her fair hair round her fingers as she blow-dried it after a quick shower and the resulting ringlets weren't quite as she'd hoped they'd be.

Halfway down the stairs she stopped to study the portrait of Annabel, and gave a sigh of regret. Apart from the long, white, muslin dress, she bore very little, if any, resemblance to the golden-curled girl who sat smiling rather provocatively from a bower of roses.

From the Great Hall of the old house wafted the gentle strains of music. No disco for Mrs Breage, Linzi remembered. That would never be in keeping with her idea of a traditional, old-fashioned Christmas. A small orchestra of five rather elderly gentlemen, wearing dress-suits, played a waltz.

The double doors were open and through them Linzi could see a swirl of colourful dancers. At least they've followed Mrs Breage's request to dress up for the evening, she observed with a growing smile of delight.

It was like stepping back in time. A Victorian Christmas card scene. Long dresses in a myriad of shades and materials created a rainbow effect, offset by the beautiful timbered background of the Great Hall.

Linzi paused in the doorway, trying to imprint it all on her memory.

'After our slight mishap this afternoon, will you trust me to steer you round the dance-floor, Lin?'

Alex was beside her, and when she nodded he placed an arm lightly round her waist to guide her forward. Within seconds her feet had followed his into the rhythm of the music and, as he drew her closer, she was aware of the slight catch of his chin against her hair and the spicy fragrance of his skin.

'That dress looks good. I had a feeling it would suit you.'

'But not quite with the same effect as when worn by Annabel,' she said, frowning ruefully.

'From her portrait, Annabel looks . . . how can I put it politely? Rather billowy and over-blown, don't you think?' he replied.

60

Linzi felt his mouth quiver against her cheek and guessed he was smiling as he continued, 'Perhaps she was trying to compete with all those roses in the bower. Or maybe the dress had shrunk a little in the wash.' He steered her skilfully round a couple of hesitant dancers. 'It looks far better on you.'

'I think you're probably being kind,' Linzi declared.

His dark eyebrows shot up. 'Why should I?'

She shrugged. 'Well, I am a bit out of my depth in these surroundings.'

'So am I,' he retorted, and she laughed as he moved his neck awkwardly in the stiff collar. 'You're forgetting, this isn't my idea of dressing at all. I'd be much more comfortable in an old pair of jeans.'

'You could have come as a hill-billy, or something,' she suggested. 'After all, it is fancy dress.'

'Now you tell me!' he said with an exaggerated sigh.

It was an evening Linzi didn't want to forget. She tried to store every moment to recall again later, and cherish. Tomorrow, she told herself forlornly, we shall be going home. Christmas will be over.

Her gaze went to Alex, looking immaculate and incredibly handsome in his borrowed dress-suit as he danced with her. The taut look about his face was gone. Yet she'd seen that haunting anguish distort his expression so many times. And always when he was with Jonathan.

Her eyes seached the room to find Morwenna, locked in Gavin's arms as they danced, and she recalled the conversation she'd overheard from the attic stairs.

'You will find someone else to love . . . and have another child,'

Jonathan was Alex's child. There could be no other interpretation of those words. Or that he still loved Morwenna.

And, having seen the sadness that filled Morwenna's eyes on occasions when she looked at him—was Morwenna's heart also still lost to him?

But now, for tonight, Alex appeared oblivious to any other woman in the room, content to dance only with her, and Linzi determined to enjoy that. Tomorrow, life would return to normal; back to London; to Morwenna and Gavin's lovely flat in Dockland.

This brief fairytale would be over.

Linzi slipped upstairs several times during the evening to make sure Jonathan was sleeping, and before she finally went to bed she crept quietly through the adjoining door into his room again.

He lay, curled under the covers, long lashes brushing his rosy cheeks, thumb resting on the pillow beside his parted lips. A perfect picture of peace, she thought, tucking the blanket a little more warmly round him.

Of all her charges, Jonathan was the most placid. Gabriella had been a strong-willed child, unsettled by all the travelling. Each time her parents moved on to a different town, Linzi had to start all over again settling the little girl into new surroundings.

Thomas had been different again. Because of Lucy's workload, her young son saw very little of her. He became entirely dependent on Linzi, fighting in protest when Lucy tried to take over. It distressed them all. Which is probably why Lucy decided to take a year or so off when she became pregnant again, Linzi reasoned as she went back into her own bedroom. What point in having children, if you saw so very little of them—and they resented you when you did?

With Morwenna and Gavin things weren't the same at all. They both were able to spend as much time as possible with Jonathan, working in their own firm as they did.

Here, staying in the family home for Christmas, it had been like a holiday for Linzi, with so many people around eager to keep the baby amused.

A thin finger of moonlight filtered in through a gap at the top of the curtains. Outside, the night was sharp with frost, giving the sky a clear star-sprinkled brilliance. No more snow had fallen during the day but had remained, crisp and deep, covering the surrounding countryside.

Once more sadness swept through Linzi as she remembered the holiday was almost over. Maybe they'd come back for Easter.

Alex had said he'd take her by boat to Frenchman's Creek when she came again.

Alex.

Her body could still feel the firm strength of his arm when they moved to the rhythm of the music. It was as if they were one. Complete unity.

Drowsily, she let her head sink more deeply into the soft pillows, and then her body jerked into wakefulness.

A thin wail trailed through the air.

Instantly, Linzi sat upright. That wasn't an owl.

The sound came again. Fretful. Wavering. The cry of a very young child. During her training she heard that same sound too many times to mistake it for anything else.

And then, from the adjoining room, came a steady rhythmic creak. Like the rock of a baby's cradle.

Linzi pushed back the duvet and stood, listening, a quiver of fear icing down her spine. I am awake, she told herself, not dreaming. Swiftly, she crossed the room towards the door separating her from Jonathan. It opened without any sound.

The room was full of shadows cast by moonlight. As she moved towards the cot, she could distinguish the shape of the sleeping baby, outlined by the soft glow of the nightlight.

Her fingers gripped the top of the wooden bars as the cry came again. This time it was louder, nearer. Stiffly, her neck turned.

Her gaze took in the high chest-of-drawers and a collection of new toys ranged along its top; the low table and chair beside it, a folded blanket lying on one arm; the wardrobe against the end wall, mirrored dressing-table beside it.

Her eyes stopped moving.

Frozen with horror, Linzi could only stare, stricken-eyed at the thin, wavering greyness rapidly creeping across the room towards her. A raw, acrid smell dragged at her throat, threatening to choke her. Her eyes watered and stung. Her mind was a turmoil of confusion.

And then she erupted into action, seizing the blanket from the chair, wrapping it round the baby, lifting him, calling out desperately for help.

The door behind her crashed open, letting in a stream of light.

Every scrap of colour drained from Morwenna's round face as she stood there, before Gavin caught her by the shoulders, pulling her back into the corridor, leaving the doorway clear for Linzi to escape.

Jonathan struggled in her arms, yelling

65

loudly, trying to free himself from the confines of the blanket, kicking out an angry protest with his feet as she ran towards the staircase calling for help as she went.

Doors were opening behind her all along the corridor; tousled heads emerging, faces pale with sleep. Voices rose in question.

'Downstairs! All of you!' Gavin commanded, and Linzi caught a glimpse of Morwenna's ashen expression as she murmured, 'The nursery wing . . . again.'

On the ground floor, Gavin directed them out onto the snowy lawn.

'Where's Alex?'

It was his mother who asked the question, and brushing off Morwenna's restraining fingers, Gavin ran back into the house.

'Get someone to call the fire brigade,' he flung back over one shoulder.

'I've already done that,' Sophie said, clutching thin elbows across her chest as she stood, shivering, in a long white T-shirt. 'It's what you're supposed to do—immediately—if you suspect a fire. I thought everyone knew that.'

'But where is Alexander?' Mrs Breage repeated and her voice rose on a high note.

As if in answer came the roar of an engine and, with blazing headlights, a vehicle shot from the back of the house and tore down the drive, tail-lights glaring red as it braked sharply at the first bend, vanishing into the darkness.

Gavin reappeared in the doorway. 'That was Alex's Land-Rover,' he said quietly, and Linzi was aware of an inexplicable movement around her, as if all the family suddenly drew together into a protective group.

'It's OK, don't worry.' Philip, his face black-streaked, joined them. 'I think I caught the fire in time.'

'For goodness' sake will someone tell me what's happened?' Mrs Breage demanded impatiently.

'There's no panic,' Philip soothed. 'The fire was in the lounge. I've done what I could in there, and shifted some of the furniture. The sprinklers came on more or less immediately, which helped.'

Linzi saw him wince slightly as he slipped his smoke-grimed hands into the pockets of his dressing-gown.

'A log had fallen onto the rug. One of the children must have unhooked the fireguard when they were in there during the evening. It toppled backwards when the log hit it and some of the embers shot out. The Christmas tree was well alight, flaming like a torch, when I arrived on the scene. Thank heavens the extinguisher worked when I tried it, but for one terrible moment I thought the fire was going to spread to the nursery above. The ceiling beams were smouldering. There was so much smoke.' He shook his head in disbelief.

Linzi saw the look that passed between him

and Gavin, and recalled Morwenna's earlier horrified whisper, *'The nursery wing . . . again.'*

A mother and child suffocated there, Alex had told her. How easily the same thing could have been repeated tonight.

She could hear the fire engine's siren as it sped up the drive from the road, while another echoed it in the distance.

'Right then, inside all of you, before we freeze,' Mrs Breage instructed, fully in command again. 'Stay in the Great Hall. That's far enough away from the lounge to be quite safe. Come along, we must stay out of the way.'

'I'll go and help the firemen,' Marcus announced firmly, and Linzi hastily caught his hand, taking him indoors with her.

But her mind was full of questions. Why had Alex left? And so rapidly, too. Had he gone for help? It seemed strange, when there were telephones all over the house. It was almost as if . . . She tried to push the idea away, but it stayed there, insidiously sliding like an evil snake into her mind.

It was almost as if he were running away.

CHAPTER SIX

'Now that all the excitement's over, everyone can go back to bed,' Mrs Breage's firm voice declared an hour or so later, when the last of the huge fire vehicles had disappeared down the drive. 'Not you, Linzi. I think you need something to make you sleep. You're as pale as a ghost. Morwenna can settle Jonathan in his cot again, although from the look of him, I doubt he'll wake until morning.' She turned to the other members of her family. 'Off you go then.'

In the warmth of the kitchen, Linzi sipped a mug of milky cocoa.

'Feeling a bit better now?'

She nodded.

'It's lucky you woke,' Mrs Breage remarked quietly. 'With all that smoke . . . it could have been nasty. Jonathan is only very young.'

'I heard a baby cry,' Linzi said slowly. 'But it wasn't Jonathan I heard. I'm sure of that.'

'No,' Mrs Breage replied. 'It wasn't Jonathan.'

Linzi shot an enquiring look at her. 'You've heard it, too?' she breathed.

'Oh, yes,' Mrs Breage answered. 'I've heard it, too.' She leaned forward and folded Linzi's hands between her own. 'Only then I didn't realise the significance. Now, I know it's a warning.'

Puzzled, Linzi stared back at her. 'A warning? What do you mean? Has something like this happened before?'

The older woman nodded sadly. 'I heard it the night Alexander's wife and little son died.'

'Alex's wife . . .' Linzi repeated the words as if trying to understand their meaning.

'Alexander married three years ago. Sarah was a local girl. They'd known each other since they were small children. Went to the same school.' Mrs Breage's eyes misted. 'They were always very close, even then. There was never anyone else for Alexander. Sarah was all he ever wanted.'

She took the empty mug from Linzi's slackening fingers and began to rinse it under the tap.

'When they finished sixth form, he joined an accountancy firm in Truro and took a part-time college course, but I don't think he was really happy there. And Sarah was eager for them to get married.' Her voice sounded regretful. 'They were far too young.'

'But they did marry?' Linzi enquired.

Mrs Breage sighed. 'Yes, eventually. My husband and I insisted they wait until they were twenty-one and surprisingly they obeyed.' She gave a faint smile. 'I must admit that I hoped they'd grow up and away from each other.'

'You didn't like Sarah?'

70

'Oh, I liked her, but somehow . . .' Mrs Breage paused while she searched for a wiping-up cloth and began to dry the mug. 'I suppose I felt Alexander should spread his wings a little. Having always been together I thought that, to Alexander, she was like another sister.' Her eyes darkened with pain. 'I was wrong, of course. Mothers frequently are. They think they know their children so well . . .' She opened a cupboard door and placed a mug inside. 'It was an idyllic marriage. I don't think I've ever seen two people so much in love.'

A sense of desolation crept over Linzi as she listened.

'They lived here,' Mrs Breage continued. 'Alexander took over as manager of the hotel when my husband died. We turned one wing of the house into a flat for them. And then Simon was born,' she said simply. 'And made a blissful marriage a perfect one. But it wasn't to last.'

Linzi saw the older woman's teeth bite hard on her upper lip.

'Simon was nine months old last June. Teething at the time. Very fretful. Sarah didn't want him to keep the hotel guests awake, so she decided to sleep in the old nursery with him that night.' Her voice faded for a second, then went on. 'The gardener had been cutting back some of the shrubs after their spring flowering that day. He'd had a bonfire during the afternoon.

'Around midnight, a wind blew in from the sea. It happened sometimes at high tide. The fire must still have been smouldering and that set it blazing again. Sparks went flying high in the air . . .' Her voice faltered again. 'It had been a hot day with a sultry, humid evening. The nursery window was open . . . there were net curtains.'

Tears brimmed on her lower lids, and Linzi heard her swallow hard before going on.

'I woke, hearing a baby cry. It was the third night I'd heard it but thought it was Simon, troubled with his teething. I took no notice. I knew Sarah was sleeping in the nursery and that she would cope splendidly. She always did.' Mrs Breage looked into Linzi's eyes. 'Only later did I realise that the cry was of a newborn child. It couldn't have been Alexander's son. But, by then, it was too late.'

'The baby and his mother suffocated?' Linzi whispered horrified, repeating Alex's words.

Mrs Breage bowed her head and a tear slid down to the corner of her mouth.

'They never woke. Never even knew what was happening. It's the only consolation I have, Linzi. It was all my fault, you see. I should have realised.'

'But how were you to know?' Linzi comforted, squeezing her hand.

'When I first heard it, I thought the cry was Simon's. It's easy to be confused when you're half-asleep.'

'I should have known,' Mrs Breage insisted, shaking her head. 'Years back, soon after the house was built in the sixteen hundreds, that wing caught fire. A nursemaid and the newly-born son of the family perished. And there have been other fires throughout the centuries. Always the same part of the house. The last was when it was bombed during the War. And . . . each time . . . someone has heard a baby crying.'

A shiver crept the length of Linzi's spine as she remembered the creak of a rocking cradle.

'The accident devastated Alexander,' his mother continued. 'I thought he'd go out of his mind. And the terrible thing is that he won't even acknowledge the tragedy. He refers to it in a completely detached way—as though it happened to someone else.'

No wonder there was such anguish in his eyes whenever he looked at Jonathan, she reflected. What must he feel, seeing another baby after losing his own little son such a short time ago; even worse to see it in the same house where the tragedy had happened?

How could I have been so wrong? Suspecting that Jonathan was Alex and Morwenna's child. Knowing Morwenna and Gavin, as I do, living with them so closely. I should have known nothing like that could have happened. Their love for each other is so plain for all to see.

Morwenna was merely showing her

sympathy towards Alex. She's that kind of person. Warm and loving. Always concerned for others. How could I have doubted that it was anything more?

'Go back to bed now, Linzi,' Mrs Breage said gently. 'I told Eve to make-up the room next to theirs, and Gavin will have moved the cot in by now. I hope you won't mind having Jonathan in there with you? After all, it's only for one night.'

Only for one night, Linzi thought despairingly. Tomorrow we all go home.

As she slipped under the cold duvet in the darkened room, she recalled the Land-Rover hurtling down the drive at breakneck speed. What agonising memories must have been aroused for Alex when he discovered fire had struck his home once more?

No wonder the shock had sent him racing away like that.

In the morning a chastened group of children eyed the sodden carpet and blackened walls and ceiling of the lounge, where most of the furniture was now pushed outside into the corridor.

'We were making pop-corn,' one of them confessed. 'The fire-guard was in the way, so we moved it back a little. Only a little bit,' he hastened to add. 'But it meant unhooking it from the wall.'

'You do know why the guard was put there, don't you?' their grandmother enquired coldly.

74

Six heads hung down, cheeks burning with colour as her scathing voice continued.

'With young children, like Marcus and Jonathan, in the house, it's put there to prevent an accident. But for your father's swift action last night, there would have been a terrible one—and little Jonathan could have died.'

'We are sorry, truly we are,' they chorused, tears brimming.

'And I could've died, too, couldn't I, Grandma?' Marcus added quickly, delighted to discover that his cousins were being told off instead of him for a change. 'I was asleep, too, wasn't I, and my bedroom's next to Jonathan's? So the flames could've roared right through the wall, couldn't they?' He waited for a moment to assess his grandmother's reaction and then went on. 'Father Christmas ought to take all their presents away for being so naughty, shouldn't he, Grandma?' His small forehead crumpled into a frown. 'Can he come and take them away, or has he gone all the way back to Lapland already?'

'Oh, Marcus!' Sophie gave an exasperated sigh. 'Do shut up.'

'But I want to know,' he protested, casting an anxious eye down at the model of Thomas the tank engine he clutched in one hand.

'Then you'd better be extra-specially good, hadn't you,' Sophie told him silkily. 'Or Father

Christmas might come back for your presents as well.'

'Sophie,' Mrs Breage said sternly, and Linzi saw she was struggling to hide a smile. 'That's moral blackmail, you know, my dear.'

'Well, I bet you won't say that if it works, Gran,' Sophie answered with a seraphic grin.

*   *   *

The snow was beginning to thaw, revealing patches of green where the lawns lay hidden, when Gavin drove them down the drive on their way home later that morning.

Clare and Philip followed in a mini-bus, which seemed to Linzi to have children's faces peeping out of every window. Eve and her husband Guy were staying on with Marcus for one more day. They stood beside Mrs Breage at the top of the stone steps, waving.

Only one person isn't there to say goodbye, Linzi reflected sadly.

'Pity we missed Alex,' David commented as they reached the ornate wrought-iron gates and turned out through them into the lane. 'He's gone over to Falmouth. Needed to have a chat with the builders about getting the lounge renovated quickly. With the first hotel bookings starting mid-January, they'll have to get down to it in a hurry.'

Linzi tried to read Gavin's face in the driving mirror. Was he covering up for his brother's absence, she wondered. Or had Alex returned to the house later in the night, and now left again on official business?

'It's such a pity,' Morwenna said and gave a final wave as the mini-bus disappeared in the opposite direction at the main road. 'Just when your mother had everything so beautiful again.' She leaned over the back of her seat to stroke Jonathan's dimpled fist, and her voice held a faint quiver as she continued softly. 'But it could have been so much worse. It's almost as though that house is fated in some way.'

'Mrs Breage told me about Alex's wife and baby,' Linzi confided.

'Did she?' Morwenna asked, twisting her head to stare at her in surprise. 'She's usually very uptight about it. Says she feels guilty, although I can't for the life of me think why. It was the gardener's fault, if anyone's, for not making sure the bonfire was out.'

'No-one was to blame,' Gavin interjected loudly. 'It was one of those disasters that happens. A series of events leading up to a terrible conclusion. If Simon hadn't been teething; if Sarah hadn't decided to sleep in the old nursery with him instead of in their own part of the house; if the shrubs hadn't been pruned that day; if the bonfire hadn't been lit; if the wind hadn't risen that night; if the window hadn't been open; if the curtains hadn't been made of a flimsy material . . . You can go on for ever, Wenna. It just happened.'

He put his foot down hard on the accelerator as the road widened. 'I just feel desperately sorry for Alex. It knocked him for six, but he won't even talk about it, Lin. Just bottles it all up inside, pretending it never happened. But last night must have brought everything back with a vengeance. You saw what an effect it had on him—rushing off like that.'

'Now you're making me feel guilty for spending Christmas there,' Morwenna groaned, running her fingers distractedly through her dark fringe. 'We did discuss it at great length, Lin,' she explained. 'And finally decided it would look very pointed if we stayed away. After all, Eve was bringing Marcus, and Claire brought all their brood.' She gave a deep sigh. 'But they're so much older and Jonathan's a baby—like Simon. It was a difficult decision, wasn't it, Gavin?'

'Don't worry, darling,' he said, patting her knee. 'Alex will get back on an even keel again.'

'But did you see the expression on his face at times?' Morwenna asked, her voice quivering a little. 'It really tore through me.'

'Don't get so upset, darling. I promise you, Alex will be all right—one day.'

But how long will that be? Linzi wondered sadly.

CHAPTER SEVEN

Ardent Andy, as Morwenna always teasingly called him, invited Linzi to visit his parents for the New Year.

'You were "on duty" with that baby all over Christmas, so I'm sure Morwenna and Gavin won't object,' he said. 'And after all I've told Mum and Dad, they can't wait to meet you.'

Linzi wondered exactly what he had told them. She and Andrew had only been to a few concerts and theatre visits together. Nothing more.

She hoped he wasn't reading too much into their friendship—for that's all it was, so far as she was concerned—and wasn't keen to go, until Morwenna persuaded her that she should.

'You haven't had a proper break away from us all since you came here in September, Lin. A week-end in Rye will do you good—especially for the New Year celebrations. You need a bit of excitement for a change,' she chided, stacking the dishes from their evening meal into the dishwasher. 'Go off and enjoy yourself. Spending all your time with Jonathan can't improve your love life.'

'Love life!' Linzi protested. 'Not with Andrew! I certainly don't want to encourage him in that way. He's not my type at all.'

'Why ever not?' Morwenna asked, putting the last saucer into the rack and closing the door. 'He seems pleasant enough.'

'Pleasant enough!' Linzi groaned dramatically. 'You make him sound like a bar of soap, Wenna.'

Morwenna chuckled. 'So what type of man are you looking for? The traditional romantic hero? Tall, dark and handsome? Don't forget, I've already snapped up the best one. There aren't a lot of them around like that, you know.'

Colour flared into Linzi's cheeks as an image floated into her mind. A tall man with unruly, dark hair—and blue eyes filled with torment . . .

Andrew's parents welcomed her with enthusiasm when she arrived on the morning of New Year's Eve.

'Never brought a girlfriend to stay before,' his father confided as he took her short, black jacket and hung it in a cupboard under the stairs. 'So we knew straight away that you must be special.'

Andrew's mother gave her a knowing smile and Linzi's heart sank. I should never have come, she thought.

'You must like children a great deal, being a nanny,' his father remarked later, as they sat down to a lunch of curried turkey. 'Looking forward to being grandparents some day in the not too distant future, aren't we, Mavis?'

'Something we've always longed for,' his wife agreed, passing a dish of diced carrots and peas to Linzi. 'We always regretted that Andrew was an only child,' she sighed, spooning chutney onto her plate. 'Little boy, isn't it, dear—the one you're looking after at the moment? Everyone seems to have a nanny these days, don't they? Can't understand how young mothers can go off and leave their children in some stranger's hands. Break my heart it would've done, if I'd had to do that with our Andrew.' Her forehead wrinkled into a frown of disapproval. 'Still, times have changed since then and they all seem to do it, don't they? Why girls bother to have babies, if all they're going to do is abandon them five minutes later, I'll never understand.' She chewed thoughtfully on a chunk of turkey, then said, 'Solicitors—the people you work for—aren't they, dear? Too busy out earning a fortune, to take care of their little one, I suppose, poor mite.'

'Morwenna and Gavin spend a great deal of time with Jonathan,' Linzi declared hotly. 'They adore him. He doesn't miss out at all. He gains, if anything. We all love him. I think he's gorgeous.'

'Can't be the same as one of your own though, Linzi,' Mrs Armstrong declared. 'Nothing makes up for having your own.' She smiled across at her son. 'Andrew's very fond of children, aren't you, love? Apart from his music, that is. Have you shown Linzi the piano in the front room? My husband and I hoped he'd take it up professionally—he's got the hands—but it wasn't to be. You're musical though, aren't you, dear? Met at a concert, so Andrew was telling us. Do you play?'

Linzi shook her head. The curry was far too biting for her even to attempt speaking.

'Never mind, dear. Perhaps, when you have a home of your own and more time . . . It is Andrew's piano, so he'll be taking it with him when he gets married, won't you, love?'

In the afternoon Andrew showed her the town of Rye. It was a fascinating place with its narrow streets and quaintly haphazard houses, built on a steep hill with the flat countryside patterning away into the distance below the ancient walls. The Christmas snow had vanished, leaving large stretches of water flooding the fields.

Turning her collar up round her ears against a biting wind, Linzi dutifully admired the church and watched the painted figurines above its clock as it struck the hour. Then, they had a pot of tea and some delicious pastries in one of the many little restaurants nearby, before they climbed the cobbles of West Street so that Andrew could show her Lamb House.

'This is where the novelist Henry James lived for eighteen years and wrote some of what I consider to be his best work,' he told her earnestly while she stood on the bend of the road, staring at the square brick building with its high flat windows and painted door.

'It's a pity it's only open from April until October or we could have gone inside. You really get the *feel* of the place then, and the walled garden is beautifully secluded.' He took her hand and drew her arm through his. 'Now you must see the Mermaid Inn. No-one can come to Rye without seeing that.'

Two of his aunts had arrived during the afternoon while they were out, and seeing them seated side by side on the sofa Linzi found herself unwillingly comparing this family with that in Cornwall. She knew it wasn't fair. There was no comparison.

Linzi guessed the aunts were sisters of Andrew's mother. All three had the same sharp chins and broad cheekbones, and their grey-tinged hair tended to fall into a similar style. She wondered if they were just visiting or had come to celebrate the New Year as well.

'You're not seeing Rye at its best at this time of year, dear,' one aunt said, delving into a plastic carrier and taking out some knitting. 'You should be here from spring onwards. The town is so pretty then. Tubs of flowers cascading around every doorway.' She lowered the knitting needles to give a conspiratorial nod towards Andrew, and continued. 'But I dare say we shall be seeing a lot more of you from now on, won't we?'

And Linzi decided it would be impolite to give a suitably crushing reply,

*   *   *

The evening seemed very long to Linzi. Andrew's mother disappeared early on to spend a great deal of time in the kitchen, refusing all offers of help. Around eight o'clock she returned, flushed and perspiring, carrying a dish of hot sausage rolls, plates of cold turkey and pickle sandwiches, and thin, crumbling slices of Christmas cake on a doily-covered glass stand.

'One of your best, Mavis,' the non-knitting sister told her, biting into a piece. 'Are you a good cook, Linzi?'

'I haven't had much opportunity to try,' Linzi replied, trying desperately not to scatter crumbs over the dark brown Dralon arm of the sofa.

'Andrew likes a nice fruit cake, don't you, love? You'll have to get Mavis to give you some lessons.'

Linzi felt tempted to ask why, but again restrained herself on the grounds of politeness.

'Now, how about a game of Scrabble, while we're waiting?' Andrew's father was delving into a corner cupboard as he spoke, and Linzi realised the remark wasn't a question, but a statement as he placed a worn box on the table.

Why are we waiting? The silly song floated into her mind, and she had to compel her expression to stay serious. It could only be for the witching hour of midnight to strike. And then . . . ?

'We always play Scrabble at Christmas and New Year,' Andrew whispered in her ear while he unfolded the board. 'It's a tradition.'

A traditional Christmas . . . Linzi could hear Mrs Breage's brisk voice. *Charades* . . . *Treasure Hunt* . . . *Fancy Dress Ball* . . .

It all seemed such an age ago. Was it only a week?

And Alex . . .

She could still recall the pressure of his arm around her as they'd danced together in the ballroom; the light brush of his chin against her forehead; smell the faint tang of spice on his skin.

Alex. How was he celebrating the New Year?

How can a man who has lost both wife and child celebrate anything? she asked herself.

And the deep sadness of his eyes haunted her yet again.

'Your turn, Linzi.' Andrew's voice broke through her reverie.

'We'll just finish this game, then I'll go and fetch the glasses,' his mother announced. 'We always have a glass of sherry to welcome in the New Year, dear,' she said, leaning towards Linzi to give her cheek a little pat. 'And what a special one this one's going to be for all of us.'

After breakfast on New Year's Day Andrew's mother suggested he took Linzi for a walk before lunch.

'I dare say you've a great deal to talk about,' she hinted. 'Dad can help me with the potatoes. I thought we'd finish up that bit of gammon today. I'll chop it and put it in some parsley sauce. That all right with you, Linzi? Not on a diet or anything, are you? Young girls like you always seem to be dieting nowadays, don't they?'

They walked down a long, flat path to the sea and as she stood, hunched, feeling the salt wind bite into her skin, Linzi couldn't help remembering the sheltered cove where tree branches reached down low to touch the water, and waves whispered softly through fronds of feathery seaweed to meet the shore.

I should never have come to Rye, she thought wretchedly, and thrust her hands deep into the pockets of her anorak away from Andrew's fingers as they brushed tentatively against hers. I don't want to be here—not with Andrew.

She closed her eyes in an attempt to drive away the vision of a tall, rangy figure standing on a snowy beach. A figure whose thick, dark hair blew caressingly across her skin as he bent his head to point out where herons nested on the far bank of the Helford River.

Momentarily, she wondered if Alex was

there, on that shingle beach, remembering, too.

But why should he ever think of me? she asked herself angrily.

'It was an idyllic marriage . . . there was never anyone else for Alexander . . . I don't think I've ever seen two people so much in love . . . and then Simon was born, and made a blissful marriage a perfect one . . .' Linzi could still hear the words Mrs Breage had spoken as they sat together in the kitchen that night after the fire.

The words seared into her and her eyes were blurred with unshed tears . . .

They left for London soon after lunch and Linzi was glad that Andrew played a Mozart tape on the car's radio cassette player for most of the journey. It meant she didn't have to talk, and she hoped he interpreted her silence as appreciation for the music. But she scarcely heard it. Her mind was far away, dreaming.

When Andrew swung the car off the road and halted it on the edge of a wood, it took a while for Linzi to notice. It was only because the cassette came to an end, its final notes dying away softly, that she realised Andrew was speaking.

'They liked you, Lin. Really liked you. All the family. I'm so glad.'

His hand moved forward and curved round her chin, drawing her closer.

'It makes everything so much easier if

everyone gets on well, doesn't it? And I want that to happen, Lin.'

Linzi felt a wave of panic sweep over her, her mind racing ahead, sensing what was to come next.

'I want to marry you.'

'But I can't marry anyone,' she protested wildly, her head jarring against the car window as she drew back. 'There's Jonathan.'

In the faint afternoon twilight she saw him smile. 'Don't worry, Lin, I wouldn't expect you to give up your job. Not at first anyway. You could still look after Jonathan. After all, it won't be for ever, will it? He's sure to go to nursery school when he's a little older. And Morwenna and Gavin don't really need you to live in, do they? They take over at night in any case.'

His mouth came towards hers and she tilted her face swiftly to one side.

'We could live nearby. I'm not sure we could afford to take on a flat like they have in the Docklands, but there must be others nearby, not so expensive. And with both our salaries . . . Please say yes, Linzi. There's nothing to stop you, is there?'

'Except that I don't love you, Andrew,' she said gently.

'But you will, Lin. Given time.'

He pressed the palm of her hand to his lips.

'We hardly know each other—is that what's worrying you? Three or four months, that's all it is, isn't it? I'm probably rushing ahead too fast for you. Always was a bit impulsive, you know. Once my mind's made up, I like to forge ahead. Get everything sorted out nicely. All cut and dried as it were. Our family are like that, you see. But not everyone's the same, are they? You probably need a bit more time to decide. Get used to the idea. And you will, Lin. Given time.'

Carefully, she eased her fingers away from his.

'No, Andrew,' she whispered. 'I don't think that will ever happen.'

The growing darkness of the car no longer surrounded her. Instead she could visualise sea stretching far away into the distance—and a man standing there on the beach, his dark hair feathering in the wind.

There was no way she could fall in love with anyone else.

CHAPTER EIGHT

'Was it a good week-end?' Morwenna demanded, rushing to the door with a wriggling Jonathan draped over one arm, when Linzi returned. 'I'm dying to hear all about it.'

Linzi pulled a wry face.

'As bad as that?' Morwenna enquired, leading the way into the kitchen. 'Look, you take Jonathan, while I put the kettle on. Gavin was complaining he's been home for at least ten minutes and hasn't had any coffee yet, weren't you, darling? Whoops—that's another new trick Jonathan's learned while you've been gone.'

She carefully removed the coffee lid from her son's questing fingers as he lunged forward in her arms.

'Hello, poppet,' Linzi said, taking the baby from her and giving him a kiss. 'So this is what you get up to in my absence, is it?'

Jonathan chuckled wickedly and made a clumsy grab at the fine gold chain round her neck.

'Come on then,' Morwenna encouraged, perching herself on the edge of the worktop. 'Tell all.'

'Have a chocolate digestive. It might sustain you if it's going to be a long story, Lin,' Gavin suggested, offering her the tin.

'There's not much to tell,' Linzi declared, taking one and letting Jonathan nibble a corner of it. 'Except that Andrew asked me to marry him.'

'And?' Gavin prompted.

'I refused, of course.'

'But why?' Morwenna questioned, dipping into the biscuit tin. 'I thought you got on so well. You seem to have such a lot in common.'

'We both like music. Nothing more,' Linzi replied flatly. 'And you can't build a marriage on just that.'

Morwenna's eyes flickered to Gavin who was filling three mugs on the other side of the kitchen.

'No,' she said, her lips curving into a smile. 'You can't build a marriage on just that.' Her fingers rested fleetingly on Linzi's arm, then were gone again. 'I'm so sorry, Lin. The trouble is, I want everyone to be as happy as Gavin and I are.'

'You have to be in love for that, Wenna,' Linzi murmured softly.

'Yes,' Morwenna agreed, reaching out to clasp Gavin's other hand as he held out a brimming mug. 'You have to be very much in love for that.'

The short, grey days of winter slowly began to lengthen as January, then February came and went. As she pushed Jonathan in his buggy along the street one morning Linzi smelled the sweet, cloying scent of hyacinths and noticed a massed row of blue and pink standing stiffly in a window-box. Soon it will be spring she reflected.

And in her mind's eye she was gazing across the sea to the mouth of the Helford river. Did the trees have now a hint of green as they swept down to meet the slow ripple of water? Was sunshine glinting on every tiny wave that caressed the shore?

Was Alex there?

Suddenly she could imagine the cool rush of air on her face, hear a sail flap before it tautened, taste salt on her lips, see the clear-cut outline of Alex's face, blue eyes smiling at her, carefree for once without their hidden shadows. Then the buggy caught its wheel on a tilted paving stone and she was jerked back to reality.

'Go bump!' Jonathan crowed beaming up at her.

He was beginning to string words together now and could already walk a few steps on his own, so that every day became an adventure for him. It was a joy to Linzi, watching his progress. He was such a bright child, constantly eager to learn something fresh.

Each day she took him to the nearby park where there were swings and a lake with several mallard and Canada geese. Even though they had yet to arrive at the iron railings bordering it, Jonathan was bouncing up and down in the buggy declaring loudly, 'See ducks.'

But as Linzi crumbled the bread she'd brought with her and gave the baby tiny pieces to throw to the clustering wildfowl, her mind was on other things.

For the past couple of weeks she'd sensed that something was troubling Gavin and Morwenna. They seemed strained and anxious all the time, and Gavin wore a permanently serious expression, making his dark good looks sombre.

Distressed by it, the previous evening, while Morwenna was pushing Jonathan's cast-off clothes into the washing machine, Linzi had tentatively asked, 'Is everything all right, Wenna?'

'Of course,' Morwenna replied brightly, then her eyes clouded. 'Oh, Lin, is it so very obvious?'

'We do all live pretty closely together,' Linzi replied, retrieving a bib from the back of the high-chair and adding it to the pile. 'It's difficult, then, to hide one's feelings. Something's wrong though, I can tell.'

'We're going to have to sell the firm, and probably the flat as well,' Morwenna wailed.

'Sell it?' Linzi exclaimed.

Morwenna nodded, her eyes filling with tears. 'You know our firm specialises in conveyancing work—dealing with the legal side of purchasing and selling houses.' She smoothed out a pair of Jonathan's tiny socks and stuffed them fiercely into the machine. 'What with the recession and everything the house market's gone into a decline—and that affects Gavin and me.' She gave a despairing shrug. 'People just aren't moving house like they used to, so who needs us?'

'But surely your firm deals with other legal matters?'

'Like divorce and probate?'

Linzi nodded.

'I persuaded Gavin to give up the divorce side years back, soon after we were married,' Morwenna explained. 'It's so emotional. You're not supposed to relate to cases, but it's awfully hard not to. Sometimes it can really tear you apart, especially when there are children involved. I hated it. And Gavin agreed.'

'But probate's all right, isn't it?'

'Wills are pretty straightforward, I suppose,' Morwenna said, adding a beaker of washing powder to the machine, 'so long as you know what you're doing, but conveyancing was our bread and butter.' Her eyes were suddenly bleak. 'It's going to be soul-destroying having to sell it all.'

'But you can't just give up everything, Wenna. It's your whole life.'

'I know,' Morwenna choked. 'But living here, in the city, is enormously expensive. The rent on the firms premises keeps going up all the time, and as for the mortgage we have on this place—it hardly bears thinking about.'

'And there's me, too, isn't there?' Linzi said quietly. 'But I don't mind taking a cut in wages. Really I don't. After all, living with you, I don't have many outgoings.'

'Don't be silly, Lin,' Morwenna protested. 'You're worth your weight in gold, coping with Jonathan the way you do.'

'But, if the firm goes and you're not working any more, you won't need me to do that, will you?'

Morwenna lowered her eyes and nodded slowly. 'That was something else we've had to take into consideration, too.' She pressed a button and the washing-machine rumbled into life, slowly filling with water.

'Do you want me to start looking for another job?' Linzi asked, feeling a sob creep into her throat.

'Not yet, Lin. Wait until after Easter. We're going down to Cornwall again then. You must come, too.'

So we are going back, Linzi thought, as she stood by the edge of the pond in the park, breaking off more bread to give to Jonathan to feed to the scrabbling ducks. But this time there was no joy in her heart.

*　　*　　*

The sadness of parting from Jonathan, as well

as Morwenna and Gavin, burned into Linzi as they followed the route to the West Country a week later. Even the idea of seeing Alex couldn't take away the pain.

Everywhere the countryside was delicately tinted with fresh green. Thick clusters of primroses were tucked under awakening hedgerows and the banks of the lane leading up to the house were deep in bluebells, their sharp musty fragrance permeating in through the open car windows.

Jonathan kept up a constant stream of chatter, excitedly pointing out everything he could see from his high seat in the car. His latest phrase was, 'What's that?' which kept Linzi fully occupied explaining, and then the new word had to be tried out and repeated again and again until something else caught his avid attention.

The house looked different without the snow that had blanketed its roof and carpeted the sloping lawns when she last saw it. Warm sunshine glowed on its walls, giving the pale grey stone an almost honey tone, and created long shadows among the lilacs and bursting rhododendrons. The whole garden seemed to exude a soft sweet fragrance.

Linzi wondered where she and Jonathan would sleep this time. Would it still be the nursery wing? However, once they were inside the front door, Mrs Breage briskly greeted her with, 'You know the way up, don't you, my dear? It's all been redecorated after the smoke blackened it so badly.'

It seemed strange to be back in the room, remembering the last time she'd been there. A faint odour of paint still hung in the air and she opened the windows wide, a gentle breeze from the sea swirling the curtains around her.

'Do you mind sleeping in here, Lin?' Morwenna asked. 'I mean . . . after all that happened.'

'No, not at all,' she lied.

Morwenna gave a little sigh and settled herself on the end of Linzi's bed. 'It's going to be much quieter than Christmas. Mother-in-law was telling me that Clare and Philip have bought an old chateau in Normandy and are staying there for the Easter holidays. They thought it might help the children with their French, so I suppose it's in his blood.' She stood up again, one hand carefully smoothing out the crumpled duvet. 'I shall miss them, but it would have been a bit crowded here with them *and* the hotel guests.' She chuckled. 'That brood really needs a hotel to themselves.'

'What about Eve and Guy—and Marcus? Are they coming?' Linzi enquired, retrieving Jonathan as he began to tug at a handle of the dressing-table drawer, and sat him on the bed.

'They were invited to go to Normandy with the others, but apparently when Marcus heard that you were coming down here, he threw a

wobbly and insisted they came, too.'
Morwenna laughed. 'You've obviously made a
hit with him, Lin. They're arriving tomorrow
afternoon. It's a pity in a way because, with
Marcus around, I doubt there'll be much
peace.' Morwenna glanced into the dressing-
table mirror as she spoke and sleeked her thick
fringe into tidiness. 'With Claire's lot, he does
tend to get lost amongst them. They all seem
to look after each other. With so many of
them, I suppose they have to.' She bent down
to remove Linzi's handbag from Jonathan as
he struggled to undo its zip and was rewarded
with a shriek of protest. 'It probably does
Marcus a great deal of good—being with
them. Knocks a few of the corners off. He is a
bit insular.' She picked up her small son and
gave him a hug. 'That's why we don't want you
to be an only, do we, my poppet? Heaven help
us if you turned out to be a dreadful child!'

Linzi was only listening with half an ear,
excitement pulsing through her at being in this
beautiful house again, knowing that Alex was
there, too.

Alex. Alex. Alex. His name sang repeatedly
in her heart.

She couldn't wait to see him again and while
Morwenna talked, her gaze kept returning to
the mullioned window, her eyes searching the
smooth green slopes of the garden below,
hoping to catch her first glimpse of him.

Maybe tomorrow, or even this evening if it

98

stayed fine, they would sail together up Frenchman's Creek. Her brow crinkled. Would he remember that promise?

With an effort she made her mind concentrate on what Morwenna was saying.

'I doubt we'll see a great deal of mother-in-law. The hotel season really gets underway at this time of year. She said they're fully booked for the next three months already.'

Does that mean that Alex, as manager, will be fully occupied, too? Linzi wondered anxiously. But not all the time. Surely he must have some part of the day free. And then . . . Her heart skipped a beat.

*   *   *

They ate dinner at a table in an alcove on one side of the dining-room. Only four places were laid Linzi noticed as she, Morwenna and Gavin sat down, after Jonathan was asleep in his cot. She waited hopefully for the fourth place to be filled, and then saw Mrs Breage make her way across the dining-room to join them, greeting each guest as she passed.

The waitress brought their starters—peppered smoked mackerel garnished with watercress, cucumber and chives.

As she began to eat, Linzi's eyes searched the room.

No untidy dark head showed way above the rest.

Perhaps, as manager, he has to organise the kitchen staff, she mused, slicing into the fish.

Mrs Breage was talking, referring to the Normandy trip. 'I really can't think why they had to buy such a place,' she sighed. 'It's huge. A monstrosity. And totally dilapidated. It'll take years to put right. Philip's got more money than sense.'

'He is an architect, mother,' Gavin put in mildly. 'If he can't restore a place like that, nobody can.'

'It needs a bulldozer taking to it from what Claire tells me,' his mother retorted, carefully removing a fish-bone with her fork and placing it on the side of her plate. 'I only hope they don't intend to move there permanently in years to come.'

'It's not the other end of the world, Mum, you could visit them easily,' Morwenna reminded her mother-in-law.

'Your holidays have always been spent here, Morwenna,' Mrs Breage said firmly. 'It's all Philip's fault. Clare would never have dreamed of going anywhere else. None of you would. Why else do I keep this place on? It costs me a fortune.'

'But you love it here, Mother,' Gavin declared. 'Be honest now.'

His mother smiled ruefully. 'It's such a millstone, I sometimes wonder if I'm doing the right thing.' Her eyes sharpened again. 'But it is your ancestral home.'

'Where's Alex?' Morwenna asked, glancing round the room. 'I thought he'd be eating with us.'

Linzi's interest quickened, then she saw Mrs Breage's mouth tighten.

'I was hoping you wouldn't ask.'

'Why?' Gavin enquired teasingly. 'Where is my infant brother? Not run away to sea like he used to threaten as a little boy, I hope.'

'You could say that,' Mrs Breage replied tersely. 'He's taken the boat and gone sailing for a few days.'

'At *Easter*'?' Gavin retorted. 'Just when everything's hotting up at the hotel? What on earth made him decide to do that?'

His mother dabbed her mouth with her serviette and made no answer.

'It's because of us, isn't it, mother-in-law?' Morwenna broke in. 'Because of Jonathan. And what happened at Christmas.'

'He didn't say so in so many words, my dear,' Mrs Breage said carefully. 'But I think he felt somewhat ashamed . . . running away like that.'

Linzi couldn't remain silent any longer, the words bursting furiously from her lips. 'How can you say that, after all that happened to his wife and baby? It must have been torture for him, seeing us all with Jonathan . . . and then that fire.'

'I think you would have great difficulty in convincing Alexander of that, my dear,' Mrs

Breage said gently. 'He sees it as a display of cowardice—he told me as much.'

'Then why has he run away yet again?' Morwenna asked hollowly.

CHAPTER NINE

It was quite understandable, Linzi kept telling herself. Alex had gone through a terrible experience. No wonder he didn't want to see any of them again.

But it didn't diminish her disappointment.

'Oh, Linzi,' Mrs Breage was saying as their empty fish plates were removed. 'I almost forgot—some friends of yours will be arriving tomorrow. The Armstrongs and their son.'

Linzi gave her a startled look.

'It was the son who phoned to make the booking,' Mrs Breage explained. 'He said you'd stayed here at Christmas and couldn't stop talking about the place. It was kind of you to recommend us, my dear.'

'Not Ardent Andy, Lin?' Morwenna said, with a gurgle of laughter. 'Surely you haven't been seeing him again?'

'No, I haven't,' Linzi snapped. 'Not since that dreadful New Year fiasco. What on earth's made him decide to come down here— and now of all times?'

'Your great enthusiasm, I should imagine,' Gavin suggested, trying to keep his mouth from smiling. 'And the thought that maybe he'd see you again. After all, he did keep trying to phone, didn't he? And Wenna and I had to keep fobbing him off with outlandish fibs as to your whereabouts.' His voice dropped to a murmur. 'After all this time, I thought we'd succeeded, too.'

'Never mind, Lin,' Morwenna comforted. 'We'll go out somewhere for the day tomorrow and avoid him, if that's what you'd prefer. It'll save you from Marcus for a while, too. Where shall we take her, Gavin?'

'How about Trelissick? The gardens there are open from Easter onwards and they'll be beautiful at this time of year, with all the flowering shrubs and bulbs in bloom. And after that, how about going over to St. Mawes?'

'Fantastic!' Morwenna agreed, turning to Linzi. 'You'll love it there, Lin. It's a delightful little place.'

But, for Linzi, the enjoyment of being in Cornwall was gone. With Andrew there, instead of Alex, nothing could be the same again.

*   *   *

At Trelissick Jonathan discovered how to roll down a hill. He was thoroughly enjoying himself toddling along the paths when a blackbird, busily hauling a long, fat, juicy worm from the finely-cut lawn attracted his attention. In his eagerness to investigate, to Linzi's horror, the baby tumbled head over heels, straight down the slope.

Momentarily, she froze, then raced after him, but Gavin's long legs went much faster, and he arrived in time to prevent his son from landing in the middle of a bed of scarlet tulips.

Jonathan gave a chortle of pleasure—then proceeded to throw himself down on the ground, and try to repeat the performance all over again, to the amusement of several onlookers.

'That, young man,' his father said sternly, picking him up and tucking him under one arm, 'is quite enough.'

'More,' Jonathan demanded, wriggling furiously to get down.

'Lunch?' Morwenna swiftly suggested and led the way back through the temptations of the National Trust shop, to the huge barn of a restaurant.

'We go across to St Mawes by the King Harry ferry,' Gavin told Linzi as they delved into pipkins of savoury beef cobbler. 'It's farther on down the lane—a chain ferry that takes cars across the Fal. You get quite a good sighting of some of the old cargo ships moored along there, but the best way to view them is from one of the pleasure cruises that run from Falmouth up river to Truro. We'll see if we can fit in a trip for you, while we're down here.'

Not quite the same as sailing in a little boat along the hidden creeks, Linzi reflected sadly.

Jonathan fell asleep in the car almost as soon as it started, exhausted by the morning's activities and a surfeit of fresh fruit salad, his round face rosy and moist as it drooped gently against Linzi's shoulder.

The soft air of the gardens, so close to the river, had made her sleepy, too, and she had difficulty in keeping her eyes open as the car bumped off the ferry and began to climb the steep winding lane to the main road that finally led down into St Mawes.

'Wake up, Lin! We're here.'

Morwenna's voice drifted into a dream of shady waters hidden beneath a canopy of dense trees, and Linzi reluctantly opened her eyes to see a wide stretch of sea where yachts and the colourful sails of windsurfers lazily drifted.

'We'll stay in the car with Jonathan until he wakes, Lin,' Morwenna whispered. 'Gavin's nodding off already and I'm dying to read his new Ruth Rendell. You go and explore the town—not that it's all that big—but there's an interesting castle right at the top of the hill with fantastic views across the Carrick Roads over to Falmouth and Pendennis castle. We'll meet you again around four at that little restaurant over there.'

'Are you sure?' Linzi asked, eyeing the sleeping baby.

'Quite sure,' Morwenna said firmly. 'Go on, before he wakes up and demands attention.'

'Jonathan, or Gavin?' Linzi enquired mischievously.

'Both of them.' Morwenna laughed.

Linzi meandered up the steep incline from the harbour, stopping every now and then to gaze into a shop window, or admire one of the pretty little cottages bordering the road.

Halfway up she leaned over the sea wall to gaze down at rocks partly-concealed by thick strands of leathery seaweed, and across the sea to the green slopes of St Anthony Head. A small ferry boat was chugging towards the jetty from Falmouth, its upper deck filled with people, and she raised a hand to wave, her mouth curving into a smile as several waved back a greeting.

Oyster-catchers dipped along the shoreline, coral-red bills contrasting brightly with their black and white feathers, rising swiftly into the air when the wake of the boat met the rocks.

The drone of bees in the heavy purple heads of a lilac bush nearby soothed the air around her, and the stone beneath her resting fingers was warm and rough with yellow lichen.

She heard the pad of footsteps come round the bend of the hill from the direction of the castle, then stop. A denim-clad arm appeared beside hers on the wall. Linzi slowly turned her head, her breath stilling.

'Hello, Alex,' she said, and her voice was ragged to her ears.

'Hello, Lin,' he replied, and she thought her heart would burst with the pleasure of seeing him again.

He hadn't changed. The thick, dark hair, blown into feathers by the sea breeze, still brushed the edge of his collar. His face was just as striking, but now lightly tanned, making the blue of his eyes more intense. She saw a nerve flicker in his cheek and wondered, was he angry?

'Are you here on your own?' he asked abruptly, his deep gaze probing hers.

She shook her head, uncertain how her voice would sound if she tried to reply. 'Gavin and Morwenna are with you?' he questioned. 'And . . . the baby?'

'They stayed in the car.' Linzi answered in a rapid gabble. 'We've been to Trelissick gardens. Jonathan fell asleep. We're meeting again at four—over there.' She pointed a tremulous finger towards the little cafe in the terrace of shops. 'I'm on my way up to the castle.' She stopped, and looked awkwardly at him, colour flaring into her cheeks. 'I know about the fire, Alex . . . and what happened. Your mother told me at Christmas.'

His jaw tightened. 'I thought she might.'

Linzi touched his hand as it lay on the wall. 'I'm sorry . . . so very sorry. It must've been terrible for you.'

'Terrible!' The bitterness in his voice tore into her, and the heads of passers-by twisted sharply in their direction. 'You really have no idea what it's like, have you, Lin, to lose those you love most in the whole world?' he stormed. 'No-one can, unless it's happened to them.'

She let his anger sweep over her, waiting until he'd finished, and then her chin jutted out as she met his furious eyes.

'Maybe I can, Alex,' she said quietly. 'Both my parents were killed in a car accident when I was five. I was with them at the time.'

His face changed in an instant, eyes closing, head lowering almost to his chest.

'Oh, Lin,' he groaned, 'I'm so sorry. I had no idea.' He raised his head again, looking straight at her. 'What must you think of me? Wallowing in my own misery like this, when all the time . . .'

'It was a long while ago now, Alex. Wounds heal, even though the scars never completely fade. Little things sometimes reopen them.'

'And that pain can be very raw, Lin.'

'I know,' she replied, and the sea blurred as she fixed her eyes on the horizon, not daring to look into his. 'We missed you at the house,' she said, needing to change the conversation.

'I'm a coward, Lin,' he retorted bluntly. 'I ran away—like I did on the night of the fire. I couldn't face seeing Jonathan again . . .'

Linzi bent her head to catch the words he said almost in a whisper.

'You see, he's so like my own child to look at. It tears me apart.'

Gavin and Alex are brothers, Linzi reminded herself. Both incredibly alike. It's natural that their sons should bear a resemblance, too. But what agony it must be for Alex.

'He's changed a great deal since Christmas, Alex. He's walking, talking—not a baby any more. Wait until you see him again.'

'I can't do that, Lin.' His tone was terse, and then his eyes were pleading with hers. 'I know you're trying to help—but it's no good. I can't see him, knowing that's how my own son would have been—if I hadn't let him and Sarah die.'

The spray from an incoming wave suddenly swept up from the rocks to chill Linzi's cheeks.

'What do you mean, Alex?'

'If I'd been awake—' He broke off shaking his head.

'You can't blame yourself for being asleep, Alex,' she declared fiercely then paused before adding softly, 'And there was no sound, was there?'

The anguish she hated so much to see returned to Alex's eyes. 'No, there was no sound . . . They suffocated, Lin. Overcome by the smoke. When . . . they were found . . . it was as if they still slept. Sarah was sitting on a chair in the nursery with the baby in her arms. Quite peacefully.' His teeth cragged at his lower lip. 'But why didn't I know?' he demanded. 'I loved them both so much. Surely some sixth sense should have alerted me?' He shook his head in despair and gave a low groan. 'I should have known.'

'The blame isn't yours, Alex,' Linzi comforted. 'It was a chain of events that no-one could foresee.'

Alex didn't appear to be listening and his voice continued as if talking to himself.

'And yet, that night at Christmas, I woke . . . I heard you cry out, Lin—but was powerless to move. Completely powerless. You and Jonathan both could have died, just like Sarah and Simon, and I was too petrified to leave my bed, dreading what I might discover if I did.'

He stared, without seeing, across the sea to where a row of trees edged the brow of a hill.

'And then I took the Land-Rover and drove as fast and as far away as I could. My only thought was to escape those flames. I didn't care what happened to Gavin's child . . . to you . . . or to anyone.' He twisted his body to face her again. 'I'm a coward, Lin. A coward in every possible way.'

'No!' she retorted hotly.

'Yes, Lin.'

Silence hung heavily between them, growing more intense with every passing second. Linzi didn't know what to say to ease his distress. She felt inadequate, wanting desperately to put her arms round him, as she would to a child, soothe him, take away the pain.

A pair of walkers came clomping down the hill from the castle at a fast pace, studded boots scraping on the Tarmac of the road, and were gone again.

'Come back to the house, Alex,' she begged. 'Be with us all. You can't run away for ever, you know.'

He made no reply.

'Time will help, Alex,' she said softly. 'The pain will lessen, one day. Please come back.'

His head lifted and she saw the stiffness of his shoulders loosen a fraction, the grim line of his mouth relaxing, and then his eyes sharpened as he gazed beyond her shoulder at the people approaching.

Linzi turned—and saw Morwenna down near the jetty, pushing Jonathan in his buggy, with Gavin a step or two behind.

In an instant Alex was gone, striding swiftly away up the hill.

'Alex!' she cried out, but it was too late. His pace increased and he was already disappearing round the bend of the road.

Why, oh, why did they have to appear now, Linzi raged, when I was so close to convincing him?

Morwenna was waving, bending to point her out to Jonathan who bounced excitedly up and down in the pushchair, calling her name.

'Did you get to the castle?' Morwenna asked.

Linzi shook her head, not trusting herself to speak.

'Are you OK, Lin? You look a bit . . . strained.'

'I'm fine,' she bit out.

Morwenna glanced at her sharply, but said no more, as Gavin jogged to catch up with them.

'Guess what?' he remarked. 'Alex's boat is moored down by the jetty.'

'Then he can't be very far away,' Morwenna replied, giving Linzi another searching look. 'We can keep an eye open while we're having tea if we sit by the window. Come on, Lin. Clotted cream, strawberry jam and scones.'

'Tea!' Jonathan shrieked, tugging at the straps confining him to the buggy. 'Me tea.'

As they went in through the low doorway, Linzi paused on the step to look back down to the harbour. There were several boats moored there, swaying on the tide. She watched as one began to move, its bright blue sail shuddering in the soft breeze as it rose.

Alex's boat? she wondered.

CHAPTER TEN

When they arrived back at the hotel, Linzi saw Andrew and his parents sitting in the garden, drinking tea at one of the little white-painted iron tables on the lawn. She hoped they wouldn't hear the quiet engine of the car as it drew to a halt at the foot of the steps.

Jonathan had fallen asleep again on the journey, but as she lifted him out, he woke and gave a long wail of tiredness. Andrew's head jerked round and his cup tilted, slopping liquid onto the grass.

'I guessed you'd be here, Lin,' he said eagerly as he stood up, and began to cross the grass towards the car.

With a sense of dismay, Linzi watched a tide of colour rise up his neck, then felt the clammy warmth of his hand close round hers.

'So this is the child . . . and its parents,' Mrs Armstrong declared acidly, studying Jonathan as she joined them.

'Yes,' Linzi replied in an even tone, although inwardly she was fuming at the scathing tone of the woman's voice. 'This is Jonathan, and Morwenna and Gavin Breage, his parents.' She turned towards them and said, 'Mr and Mrs Armstrong . . . and Andrew.'

'I must talk to you alone, Lin,' Andrew blurted out. 'Can we walk down to the sea? I found the path a while back while I was mooching around.'

'I'll have Jonathan,' Morwenna said quickly, stepping forward, ignoring the imploring look that Linzi gave her. 'Don't rush back, Lin. Gavin and I'll put him to bed. Do please excuse us, Mr and Mrs Armstrong, but our son's had rather a long day and it's way past his bedtime.'

'I really have nothing to say to you,' Linzi protested while Andrew led her down through the garden, a fragrance of pine rising up as they trampled on the thin dry brown needles strewing the path. 'Why on earth did you come here?'

'To see you, Lin,' he replied. 'Why wouldn't you answer my phone calls and letters? You must realise by now how much I want to marry you.'

Linzi gave a weary sigh. 'I've already told you, Andrew. I don't love you.'

'But how can you be so sure, Linzi,' he persisted, 'when you won't even let me near you?'

'Just take it that I do, Andrew,' she said. 'And it was far better to make a clean break. I don't want you to be hurt.'

They had reached the cove now, shingle sliding beneath their feet as they stepped through the gap in the wall and descended the steps. Linzi breathed deeply, drawing in the cool salt air, trying to relax her tense body.

115

The tide was high and large waves thundered up the shore, then receded with a rattling drag of tiny stones. Far out, a yacht was slicing through the water, heading towards the Helford river, its deep blue sail taut.

'But I am hurt, Linzi,' Andrew retorted. 'How can I be otherwise?'

Linzi's eyes watched the boat turn slightly, its sail whipping across as it leaned into the wind, sea creaming high on either side of its bow.

'Are you listening to me, Lin? I want us to continue as we were. Just friends to start with . . . going to concerts . . . plays . . . like we used to . . . and then, given time . . .'

A high-pitched shriek of delight shrilled out, making Linzi spin round.

'Marcus!' she cried, and was glad of his timely arrival.

The little boy came running over the shingle towards her, his feet slipping in their haste so that he landed flat on his stomach, then scrambled upright as Linzi reached him.

'I didn't want to go to France for Easter,' he gabbled, bending to rub bits of dried seaweed from his knees. 'All those others have gone to live in a castle in Norman's sealand. Mummy and Daddy and me are all going on Tuesday, after it's been Easter, but I don't like castles. There's ghosts and enormous spiders and lots of very horrid things in castles and you don't have any lights, only candles, and the wind sometimes blows them out.' He patted the pocket of his jeans and gave Linzi a wicked smile. 'I've got some real matches for when we do go there.'

'Then I think you'd better let me look after them for you, Marcus,' she said, holding out her hand for them. 'Matches are far too dangerous for a little boy like you to have. You could hurt yourself really badly.'

The child pushed out his lower lip. 'I'm not little,' he muttered, then, after scrabbling in his pocket for a moment or two, reluctantly dropped half-a-dozen matches into her waiting hand.

'Is this another of your charges?' Andrew enquired stiffly, starting to climb the short flight of steps from the beach. 'I thought there was only Jonathan.'

'No, this is Gavin's nephew,' she replied.

'Does that mean there'll be a whole horde of children here? If I remember correctly, after your visit at Christmas you said his sisters had gathered quite a collection from various marriages.'

'That wasn't quite what I said, Andrew. Anyway, there's only Marcus this time, the others are in Normandy.' Linzi caught hold of Marcus by the hand. 'Let's go back and have some dinner, shall we?'

'And then you can read to me, like you did before,' Marcus announced firmly. 'Or else I might get nasty dreams. My bedroom's right at the top of the stairs, next to Jonathan's, same as last time we came, so you'll know where to find me.'

Morwenna and Gavin went out with Eve and Guy to visit old friends later that evening and, to avoid Andrew, Linzi decided to have an early night. After a day spent in the sea air, she felt quite tired in any case, but there was an uneasy prickle down her spine as she checked Jonathan in the adjoining room before she settled into her own bed. She hadn't forgotten the previous occasion he'd slept in the nursery—or the eerie cry she'd heard.

Was it all my imagination? she wondered. And yet, Mrs Breage insisted she'd heard the same sound—on the night Alex's wife and child died.

It's so different now, Linzi thought, looking out at the garden scented by the flowering currant bushes that grew below her bedroom window as she closed it. Then, snow had covered everything, but tonight a froth of blossom, pale in the half-light, scattered the lawn. Almond, or is it cherry? she mused, studying the shapely trees.

Her ears were tuned for any noise when she slipped into bed and switched off the bedside lamp, but all she could hear was the sea surge softly, tugging at the shingle as if reluctant to leave the shore. It soothed her swiftly into sleep.

The cry came. Strident. Forceful. Penetrating the shroud of darkness that seemed to smother her. Her breath was trapped as though a heavy weight sat upon her chest, pinning her down. Her eyes stung and hcr lips rcfuscd to part.

Linzi tried to lift her head from the pillow, but instead it lolled sideways.

Air. The window. Her brain was sluggish, unwilling to form thoughts. Her body refused to obey.

Again she heard the cry. Not a strange child, but Jonathan.

Jonathan!

She had to reach Jonathan. Her limbs strove to move—but remained lifeless.

Jonathan . . . I must reach Jonathan.

The room was spinning, faster, faster. She was lost in a deep whirlpool that tightened around her chest, sucking out every scrap of breath.

The voices were growing louder, echoing, merging as she spun round and round in a vortex, not knowing where she was or where to go.

Alex.

The name crept past her lips and whispered into the smoke-filled air.

'It's all right, Lin. I'll have you out of here in no time.'

Linzi moved her neck stiffly and her cheek brushed against the cool metal of a button.

Slowly, her questing fingers reached upwards and touched the warmth of skin, then the smooth sleekness of hair.

'Alex?' she croaked, forcing her eyes to open.

His face was smudged, the dark hair clinging to his forehead, but in the strange shimmering brilliance of light that surrounded them, his eyes smiling back into hers, clear and blue.

She struggled as he lifted her. 'Jonathan! Where's Jonathan?'

'He's fine, Lin,' came Alex's calm reassurance. 'We'll be with him in a moment or two.'

Linzi let her eyelids close again, content to be held in Alex's arms while he carried her, hearing the comforting throb of his heart through the rough denim of his jacket. 'How did the fire start?' she murmured.

Alex didn't answer and from the terrifying roar of noise that assaulted her ears, she realised they were outside her bedroom door now, heading away from the inferno. As the air cleared slightly and became easier to breathe, he spoke again.

'Marcus had some matches . . .'

'But I took them away from him!'

'He obviously had more tucked away then . . . and his duvet caught alight.'

'Oh, no!' she gasped horrified, raising her face away from his shoulder. 'Is he all right?'

Alex gave a short laugh. 'That little monster has nine lives. Not that he deserves any of them . . . after this.' His grip tightened round her. 'He'd hidden himself under Jonathan's cot, when I eventually found him.'

'You did come back to the house, after all,' she said, her voice fighting through the dryness of her throat.

'And thank goodness I did. You see, when I returned to the boat after I'd seen you over at St Mawes, I couldn't forget what you said, Lin . . . I realised you were right. I can't keep running away. Sarah and Simon are dead. I have to face up to that . . . but life has to go on.' She heard his tone change to a different note. 'I'd just moored down in the cove and was climbing the path to the garden, when I noticed flames behind the glass of one of the upper windows . . . It was like reliving a nightmare . . . I wanted to turn and run, go back to the boat . . . anywhere . . . but then I knew it was impossible. You were in that house, Lin—and Jonathan. I couldn't leave either of you there . . .'

His lips brushed across her hair as he adjusted her weight in his arms. 'Everyone was downstairs on the other side of the house when I reached the hallway . . . they had no idea . . . and by then the top of the staircase outside Marcus's room was already ablaze.'

Linzi twisted her head. Shadows seemed to leap and dart around her, patterning the pale

121

walls.

'Where are we?' she asked, clinging on to him.

'At the end of the corridor, climbing the back stairs to the attics.'

She saw his mouth tighten into a grim line.

'The fire's taken quite a hold with all the old beams and woodwork in this place, but there's nothing for you to worry about. They'll have us out in no time.'

Panic flared through her. 'Jonathan . . . and Marcus?'

'They're up there already, and they're fine, Lin. Truly they are.' His long fingers soothed across her forehead. 'Jonathan started crying as soon as I picked him up, which was a relief, although Marcus is a bit subdued. Even so, I had a job persuading him to stay up there with the baby, while I came back for you, but eventually he agreed. He's a plucky little chap, you know, Lin. Wanted to come back down and save you all by himself!' He pushed open a door with one shoulder. 'Now, are you fit enough to stand?'

With his arm supporting her shaking body, Linzi slid her feet to the ground, her bare toes meeting the cold linoleum covering the floor, and was instantly knocked sideways as a sobbing Marcus threw himself at her, hugging her knees.

'I didn't mean to catch us all on fire, Lin,' he wept. 'Only that baby's crying woke me up and

122

I thought it was Jonathan and it was all dark so I lighted one of my matches . . .'

'Careful, young man!' Alex warned, holding her steady as she bent to comfort the little boy. 'Let's have Jonathan.' He picked up the baby who was sitting, silently sucking his thumb, and placed him in Linzi's waiting arms, glancing swiftly across the room as he did so. 'I think we'd better try the skylight.'

Smoke was already starting to drift in under the door, rising in wispy tendrils to eddy round them. Cuddling Marcus and the baby close, Linzi watched Alex drag a high chest-of-drawers away from the wall and manoeuvre it under the tiny window, then climb up.

At first the hasp refused to budge as he heaved at the window, but finally it gave way, showering Linzi with flakes of old white paint as it shot open and the cold night air rushed in.

'You'll have to go through first, Lin, then the children.'

He jumped down and took the baby from her, while she scrambled up on to the wooden top of the chest-of-drawers.

'Steady!' he warned, gripping her ankle as she rose cautiously to a standing position. 'You're doing splendidly. Can you reach?'

With a horrifying whoosh of flame, the door burst open, and Linzi screamed out in terror, Marcus echoing her cry as Alex swiftly lifted him up beside her.

'It's OK, Lin. You've plenty of time. Grip

the edge of the window-frame and heave yourself through.'

Linzi's fingers scrabbled—frantically at the edge of the skylight, splinters digging into her nails as she gripped it, then she was out in an undignified heap on the slate tiles of the roof, under a starlit sky.

Looking down, she could see the fire was already searing its way across the little room, consuming the linoleum at a furious rate. Any moment it would reach the chest-of-drawers and the ancient wood would vanish in a trice.

'Take Marcus! Quickly!' Alex's voice was urgent as he thrust the little boy upwards with one hand and she dragged him through, the child's arms clinging frantically to her neck.

'I can hold on to the chimney, so you can have Jonathan,' Marcus declared, quickly pulling away from her to clutch at the bricks of the stack.

'Hang on very tight then,' she ordered and leaned back through the window to catch hold of the baby as Alex held him. As she did, her feet slid away from her, scraping downwards over the smooth slates, then were caught by the guttering.

'Alex!' she cried out, desperately hauling herself back and lifting the crying baby through the skylight, her gaze filling with horror as, with a tremendous roar, the room below erupted into flame. Trying to pacify Jonathan as she held him with one arm, while the other gripped Marcus against the chimney, there was no way she could help Alex to climb out.

For one agonising second it was as if time hung suspended, then with a slither, the long, denim-clad body wriggled through the narrow opening and was sitting high up on the roof slates beside her, slapping vigorously at the smouldering legs of his jeans.

'Oh, Alex!' she breathed in a huge sigh of relief.

'So there you all are,' a cheery voice exclaimed and, to their startled eyes, the dark outline of a fireman appeared farther along the roof. 'Now, who's going to be first down?'

'Me! Me! Me!' Marcus shrieked, letting go of the chimney stack to slide down the roof and be caught safely before he reached the edge.

'Don't any of you go away, will you?' the fireman joked, giving them a broad wink. 'I'll be back as soon as I've handed this young man over.'

While they waited, braced against the chimney stack, Alex smoothed one finger over the top of Jonathan's silky head while the now quiet baby contentedly chewed the collar of his denim jacket.

'After . . . my wife . . . and Simon died,' he told Linzi slowly, 'I thought I could never touch or hold a baby again. And, when you all came here at Christmas and I saw Jonathan, it

125

was unbearable. It brought back so many memories of both of them. I couldn't believe the pain. I loved them so very much, you see.'

His hand rested lightly over hers and Linzi felt his fingers tighten. His hair, ruffled by the wind, softly feathered her cheek, making her heart ache with longing as he said, 'One day, maybe . . .'

'Right then, m'dears.' The fireman was back, interrupting Alex's words. 'Let's have the little one next. Are you two all right to follow me down?'

*   *   *

What remained of that part of the house, was only a shell; its outer walls still intact and standing; the whole of the interior completely destroyed.

'I shan't have the nursery wing rebuilt,' Mrs Breage commented sadly the following day, when the family stood viewing the ruins. 'This has finally decided me. There's been too much tragedy over the years.' Her eyes met Linzi's. 'It must never be repeated . . . And I don't ever want to live here again.'

'But, Mum,' Morwenna remarked, 'you won't leave Cornwall, will you? You love it so much.'

'Oh, no, I shan't do that, my dear.' Mrs Breage smiled. 'I intend to sell up; buy something far smaller. There's been a property

126

developer dogging my heels for months, wanting to turn the place into sheltered accommodation. They make a fortune from that sort of thing nowadays, you know. And this is an ideal position. He offered a ridiculous price, so I must see how all this fire damage is going to affect things.' She gave them a shrewd look as she said, 'After all, none of you really wanted to take on the house, did you? And with Gavin and Morwenna moving down here in any case . . .'

Linzi glanced at Morwenna with raised eyebrows.

'Gavin's come up with a brilliant idea, Lin,' she said, linking arms to walk down the garden. 'I don't know why we didn't think of it before. There's quite a demand for property around here, with all the new roads making Cornwall so much more accessible. What with conservation and everything, dozens of lovely old buildings and barns are being restored and there's a growing stream of holiday visitors wanting to rent.'

'So what *is* Gavin's idea?' Linzi demanded, hitching Jonathan more comfortably on to her hip and disentangling his questing fingers from the gold chain round her neck.

'Didn't I say?' Morwenna asked, pushing her fringe away from her eyes as the sea breeze fluttered it across her face.

'No, you didn't!'

'Oh, Lin, we're going to buy a place near

here—probably over at St Mawes as we love it so much,' she declared eagerly, 'then start up a new firm and see what we can make of it.' Her round face lost some of its excitement. 'But it's you we're worried about, Lin.'

'I'll find another job,' Linzi said quickly, catching Jonathan's chubby hand as he snatched at the deep purple flowers of a rhododendron bush that blazed beside the path.

'We were hoping you'd stay in Cornwall with us,' Morwenna suggested cautiously. 'You see . . . oh, Lin, we don't want to lose you! And now that I'm pregnant again . . .'

'You're what?' Linzi cried out, startling Jonathan so much that he frowned up at her and said in a reproving tone, 'Noisy!'

'Well, only just.'

'Of course, I'll stay,' Linzi exclaimed in delight, her eyes catching sight of a boat moored down by the rocks in the cove.

Morwenna followed her gaze and smiled as she held out her arms for her son. 'I'll take Jonathan back to the others now, but you'd better stay, Lin. That's Alex's boat out there.'

Her heart pounding with excitement, Linzi ran the rest of the way along the path, through the gap in the flintstone wall, down the steps, over the shingle, her feet crunching on dried seaweed, and then, at the water's edge, slipped off her sandals to step into the shimmering wavelets that crinkled the shore.

The blue-sailed boat skimmed the edge of the sand, turning as it did, and Alex reached out, catching her round the waist with one strong, tanned arm, to lift her effortlessly over the side.

Her dress clung wetly to her legs, but Linzi was oblivious to that. The movement of the boat had tipped her sideways as it swung away from the shore so that she was held firmly by Alex, and for one intoxicating minute he seemed reluctant to let her go.

A flurry of wind sent her hair into a wild tangle around her cheeks, and she tried unsuccessfully to brush it away as Alex leaned forward, cupping her chin with one hand while he kissed her lightly on the lips, and she could taste the salt of the sea.

Once the boat was in calmer waters, sailing up the wide Helford river, Linzi sat on the varnished wood of the seat and looked around her, while Alex steered.

A pair of shelduck, bright in their chestnut, white and black plumage, bobbed nearby, scarlet-beaked heads turned warily to watch them pass.

Alex pointed towards the trees bordering the bank. 'There's the heronry,' he said softly.

And she heard the heavy flap of wings as one slender grey bird rose into the air, before swooping down to the mudflats along the river's edge and began to strut, sentinel-like, on long thin legs through the shallow water.

'Where are we going, Alex?' she asked, not really caring so long as she was with him.

He smiled, and she saw the lines of pain ease from around his mouth, the cleft in his cheek deepening, his clear, blue gaze meeting hers in a way that sent her pulse racing as he said quietly, 'Into the future, Lin. Our future.'

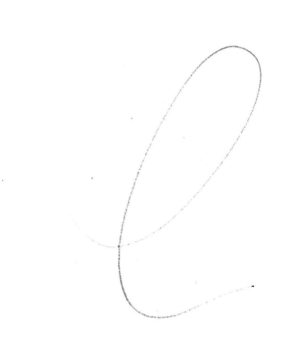